Cautiously Brian jabbed the stick into the pile of clothes — and before his eyes the clothes began to gather into themselves — whirling, twitching furiously until they took on a hunched, human shape. Brian swallowed. The monster was beyond ugly.

"Puh-leeze!" the monster said, its voice raspy and choked. "I have to get back under the bed before the sun totally rises."

"No way!" said Brian. "You wrecked my bike. You've been pulling stuff, trying to get me in trouble."

"That's my *job*!" the monster croaked.

LITTLE MONSTERS

A novelization by A.L. Singer
Based on the motion picture screenplay written by
Terry Rossio & Ted Elliot

SCHOLASTIC INC.
New York Toronto London Auckland Sydney

ISBN 0-590-42742-3

12 11 10 9 8 7 6 5 4 3 2 1   9/8 0 1 2 3 4/9

Printed in the U.S.A.   01

First Scholastic printing, August 1989

Chapter 1

They were arguing.

Again.

Brian's mom and dad were like a broken record — especially since the move to the new house. A dream house, they called it, but there was always something to fight about — the plumbing, the wallpaper, the insulation. . . .

Not that they were *bad* people, Brian kept telling himself. Just tired and cranky from working too hard. And at least they didn't argue in front of their sons — well, *usually*.

This time Brian was in the room with them — and something was terribly wrong. They just didn't look like themselves.

For one thing, Mr. Stevenson's face had turned into a TV set.

"Holly, can't you see I'm exhausted?" he said to his wife. The picture on his face kept changing — Larry Bird twisting in for a lay-up, the Patriots at the four-yard line with first and goal, Roger Clemens uncorking a fastball. . . .

Brian tried to scream at him, tell him what was wrong, but no words would come out.

"But it's been almost a month since we moved here, and you haven't lifted a finger!" Mrs. Stevenson scolded.

Didn't she *see* what was happening to him? Brian looked desperately at his mom — and his jaw fell open in shock. A giant hammer had replaced her right arm, a vacuum cleaner was where her left leg used to be, and an enormous steel-wool pad began to grow from her head.

Suddenly Mr. and Mrs. Stevenson fell silent. They turned slowly to Brian. He backed away. With stiff, zombielike steps they approached him, their words overlapping.

"Did you clean your room, pal?"

"Is that *your* mud you tramped into the house?"

"I don't care if your brother used the peanut butter last — put it away!"

"You're twelve years old, Brian, you should know better!"

The TV crackled. Mom's vacuum-cleaner leg whirred. Go away! Brian wanted to shout. Leave me alone! . . .

CAUTION.
CAUTION.
CAUTION.
Brian blinked awake. In the darkness, two amber

lights flickered their warning. He could hear his mom and dad but couldn't see them.

It was a dream. A dream! He told his heart to stop beating so fast.

His eyes focused on the caution lights, then followed the wires that snaked out from underneath them. The wires led down to two metal plates on his alarm clock — plates that had been screwed in where the alarm bells once were. Each time the clock's hammer pecked away at the plates, it completed an electrical circuit that made the lights flash.

Brian smiled. He'd put those plates there himself. It was a perfect way to set off an alarm without anyone else knowing.

Like his parents.

Rubbing the sleep out of his light brown eyes, he sat up. His blue striped pajamas were wrinkled, his dark hair bunched to one side. But those things didn't matter. It was past everyone's bedtime and the house was his!

He turned the alarm off and flicked on his nighttable lamp. Swinging his legs off the bed, he grabbed a pair of thick wool socks and put them on. They would be perfect soundproofing against the hardwood floors.

Like a skater, he slid silently across the room, past his cluttered worktable. Then he lifted the door up out of the floor and let a feeling of freedom wash over him. Even though an attic room was great for privacy, sometimes it got a little lonely.

He grabbed the banister with both hands, lifted

his feet, and slid down. At the bottom he dropped silently to the floor.

On tiptoe, he sneaked down the hallway, past his brother Eric's bedroom. From the end of the hall he could hear voices from his parents' room. They were arguing, just as they had been in his dream.

"You can't expect me to commute two hours a day, then come home and *spackle!*" his father's voice boomed. "I *hate* spackling."

"No one's holding a sandblaster to your head, Glen," Mrs. Stevenson replied, her voice sharp with sarcasm. "Do what you want. Maybe you should just sleep in your suit."

They were good for another half hour at least, Brian decided. No *chance* they would discover him.

He scurried to the top of the stairs. Below him, the living room and kitchen lay waiting. Carefully he placed a foot on the first step down.

CRRRRRREAK.

Brian froze. He lifted his foot and slowly dropped it to the left.

Silence. He shifted all his weight onto the foot. Then, like a soldier stepping through minefields, he made his way around the cricks and cracks, all the way to the first floor.

When he saw the kitchen, his stomach began to rumble with hunger. And there was one way to deal with *that*. . . .

In a flurry of motion, Brian grabbed everything he needed from the cupboards and drawers.

It was a snap. A slice of bread, a thick smoosh

of peanut butter, a tangy layer of raw onion, another bread slice — the best sandwich this side of heaven!

Brian looked at the clock. It was twelve twenty-seven — perfect timing, as usual.

He ran into the living room and pulled the TV cabinet close to the couch. Making sure to press the mute button, he grabbed the remote controller and flopped back into the cushions. He adjusted himself left and right, settling in. Pretty comfortable for a sofa bed, he thought.

With a flick of the remote controller, the TV lit up. A smile crept across Brian's face. He raised the volume ever so slightly, so he could just hear it. Then, finally, he allowed himself to relax.

Nothing, *nothing* in the world could beat this, Brian said to himself. No parents to make him feel guilty, no whiny little brother. Just him, some great food, and David Letterman. Perfect.

Except for one thing.

There was a shadow moving behind him. A strange, hunched shadow. It started in the kitchen and slinked across the living room. One move of the head, one glance over his shoulder, and Brian might have seen it. He might have even scared it away.

But as it shot up the staircase, Brian's eyes never left the TV.

Chapter 2

"*Late Night* will not be seen tonight — " came the TV announcer's voice.

Brian sat up, his mouth stuffed with peanut butter and onions. "Whaa — ?"

"Instead, WXRB TV is proud to present this special community service broadcast — "

"EEEEEAAAAAAGHHHH!"

The scream made Brian leap out of the sofa. It pierced through him like a knife.

There was no doubt where it came from — Eric's room. Brian quickly turned off the TV, slid it back into place, and raced for the staircase.

Glancing up, he noticed that Eric's door was open. He could have sworn it was shut moments ago. He scrambled up the stairs.

But he put on the brakes when he saw his mom and dad. With concerned looks on their faces, they rushed down the hallway and into Eric's room.

Brian hid in the shadows. He wasn't going to get

in trouble just because his brother had had a stupid nightmare.

Upstairs, Eric was shaking. In all his nine years, he had never seen anything so scary. He wondered if his light brown hair had gone gray with shock.

When his parents came rushing in, he blurted out, "Mom! A monster!"

Mrs. Stevenson sat down on the bed next to him. She gave him a gentle stroke on the cheek. "Honey, are you okay? Were you having a bad dream?"

"I was wide awake!"

Mr. Stevenson smiled.

"It's no joke, Dad," Eric insisted. "It was a real monster!"

"Honey," his mom said reassuringly, "there are no monsters."

They're not getting it, Eric thought. They don't believe me. "It ran in from the hall, grabbed my ankle, and slid under my bed!"

"Under your bed?" His dad's eyes seemed to light up. *Finally* one of them was listening!

Mr. Stevenson knelt down on one knee. He reached under the bed and swept his arm back and forth.

A wave of fear shot through Eric. "No, Dad! *Don't!*"

His dad just smiled back.

Then, without warning, his arm began to jerk. He let out a helpless grunt as his eyes filled with terror. He struggled to pull away but couldn't. Mrs.

Stevenson's face lost its color. Eric thought he would faint.

And just then, Mr. Stevenson yanked his arm out — attached to a pair of Eric's dirty underwear. On his shirtsleeve, several dust balls dangled.

"See?" he said with a grin. "No monsters."

Eric gulped. That *wasn't* funny.

His mom still looked a little pale as she picked the dust off Mr. Stevenson's sleeve. "You see, Eric, all the dust bunnies scare them away."

"Bunnies?" Eric glanced down under the bed.

Mr. Stevenson rolled his eyes. "There are no bunnies, there are no monsters. There's *nothing* under your bed, so you can go to sleep now!"

"Can I have a flashlight?" Eric asked.

"Sure, honey," his mom replied. "Dad'll get it."

His dad shot her a stern look. "Holly, if we humor him — "

But Mrs. Stevenson's angry glare cut him off.

"All right," he finally said. With a shrug, he turned to leave.

Before Mr. Stevenson's shadow was in the hallway, Brian had bolted up the attic stairs and into his room.

Now Eric and his mom were alone. With a warm smile, she pulled the covers over him. "You know, I'll bet the monsters are more afraid of you than you are of them. Once you realize they don't exist, they're gone." She tucked him into the bed. "That's a lot of power."

Grown-ups are strange, Eric thought. Instead of listening to you, they always try to teach you some lesson that doesn't make any sense.

When Mr. Stevenson returned to the room with a flashlight, Eric felt better. He took it under the covers and clutched it tightly.

"Take it easy on the batteries, okay?" his dad said.

"I will," Eric answered.

He could feel his eyelids getting heavy as his parents said good night and left the room.

Upstairs, Brian could hear the whole thing. His mom and dad were in the hallway now, whispering. He pressed his ear to the floor and listened.

"Do you think Eric heard us arguing?" his dad asked.

"Of course," his mom answered. "That's what scared him."

In his attic room, Brian softly closed his door. What a place this house was, he said to himself with frustration. Parents who fight about spackling, a brother who sees monsters in his room. . . .

One thing Brian knew for sure. It was tough for a guy to get any privacy in this place.

The next morning, Brian sat up suddenly in bed. Bad dreams again. This time he had been surrounded by the kids in school — Ronnie Coleman, Jim Mignogna, a dozen others. The tough guys, the ones who wanted to make sure that any "new kid" in school knew his place — at the bottom of the heap. In the dream, their teeth had grown sharp points, their skin huge black moles.

Brian rubbed his eyes and tried to wipe the image from his mind. He pulled on his clothes and slung his backpack over his shoulders. Then he raced down the two flights of stairs and headed for the kitchen. Breakfast time always put him in a good mood.

At least it *usually* did. This morning something was up.

He slowed down as he walked in. No one looked up at him. His mom packed the dishwasher while his dad busily looked over some papers for work. Eric kept his head down, shoveling cereal into his mouth.

Brian looked around, puzzled. He sat down quietly next to Eric.

His dad was the first to break the silence. "I hope whatever you watched last night was worth your allowance and two weeks of TV."

"Huh?"

"We found the sandwich," his mom said, turning on the dishwasher.

Brian gulped. He knew he'd forgotten about *something* the night before. "What sandwich?" he asked feebly.

His mom looked him in the eye. "Brian, you are the only human being in this house who eats peanut-butter-and-onion sandwiches."

"Every time you get caught, you think you can

lie your way out of it," his dad added.

Brian felt his face turning red. It was all Eric's fault, he told himself. If Eric hadn't screamed like a big baby, Brian would have finished the sandwich. No one would have known a thing —

CLANK-CLANK!

Brian's eyes darted toward the noise. Above the kitchen sink, water pipes showed through a hole in the wall. They shook with each clank. Mrs. Stevenson quickly turned the hot water faucet on and off.

The noise stopped, and Mrs. Stevenson sighed with relief.

CLANK-CLANK . . . CLANK!

This time the noise kept up, even after Mrs. Stevenson turned the faucet. Thinking fast, she shut off the dishwasher.

"Augh! This *house*!" she shouted.

Mr. Stevenson put a comforting arm on her shoulder. "The plumber will be out next week."

"Can I leave *him* the dishes?" Mrs. Stevenson asked.

With a smile, Mr. Stevenson leaned against the cupboard. "Just keep saying to yourself, 'It's our dream house. . . .' "

"It's our dream house . . . It's our dream house. . . ." Brian noticed his mom was calming down, starting to believe what she was saying. "It's our dream house!"

CLANNNK!

A deep depression settled over Mrs. Stevenson once again.

Mr. Stevenson suddenly jerked his arm away from the cupboard — and it had nothing to do with the water pipes. It had to do with the soupy pink goop that had dripped onto his shirtsleeve.

"What the — ?" He yanked open the cupboard door. Inside, on a stack of dishes, lay a soggy half-gallon container of melted strawberry ice cream.

Eric began to giggle. And Brian had to admit, it *was* pretty funny. He tried to hold back a laugh, but couldn't.

His father's furious glare was like a laser. It wiped the smile off Brian's face. "You're dead," he said.

"I didn't do it!" Brian shot back.

"Just like the sandwich." With disgust, Mr. Stevenson plucked the carton out of the cupboard.

"Okay, it was my sandwich," Brian admitted, "but I didn't have any ice cream! You always blame me for everything — "

"*Somebody* puts scuff marks on the door whenever he kicks it open," his mom interrupted. "And *somebody* sticks gum under the table!"

Brian shook his head. "Not me."

"Brian, you're old enough to know the difference between right and wrong," his dad said. "Start acting like it."

This was a frame-up, Brian thought. He remembered opening the cupboard the night before, and there was *definitely* no ice cream there.

There was only one person who could have done it. Not that it mattered — Brian's parents would never believe it. All Brian could do now was shut his mouth. But as he lowered his eyes dejectedly, he promised himself one thing.

Eric was going to pay for this.

Brian slumped off to brush his teeth. In his mind, he turned over all kinds of ways he could get back at Eric — yanking down his pants in front of the girls, throwing his books under the bus. . . . For once, Brian was actually looking forward to school.

But it didn't take long for those old feelings to come back. Feelings that none of the kids in school really wanted him there.

He sat dejectedly on the stairway. As usual, Eric had left early to walk to the bus stop with his friend Todd — at least *he* had friends. And as usual, his dad was hurrying off to work, complaining that he was late.

Soon only Brian's mom was left in the house. She walked toward the kitchen, not noticing Brian.

"Mom," he said softly, "can I stay home from school?"

Mrs. Stevenson turned around. A sympathetic smile crossed her face, and she walked up the stairs to sit next to Brian. "It's not easy being the new kid on the block, is it?"

"I hate it here," Brian replied.

"You miss your friends, don't you?"

"Ma . . ." Brian didn't know how to put it. He looked helplessly into his mother's eyes. "It's killing me!"

He could tell she understood. She put her arm

tenderly around his shoulder. "Doesn't Mr. Coleman, the realtor, have a son in your grade?"

Brian sneered. "Ronnie Coleman is a toad."

"He seems like a nice kid."

"Then *you* invite him over for milk and dead flies."

"Brian, we've only been here three weeks. You have to give it some time. *Eric's* made some pals."

"Eric's Eric."

SCREEEEEEEK!

They both sprang to their feet at the loud scraping noise from outside. Brian ran for the door to the garage.

But his dad opened it before he got there. Brian could practically see steam coming out of his ears. He grabbed Brian's hand and led him through the garage and past his idling Mazda GLC. Behind them, Mrs. Stevenson stood at the door and watched.

They stopped just beyond the car. There, lying on the driveway like a giant, crushed metal spider, was Brian's ten-speed bike.

Brian's mouth fell open in disbelief. What was going on here — did his dad do this on purpose? Was this some crazy way of getting back at him for the sandwich? He looked at his dad, baffled. "You ran over it."

"Guess why?" Mr. Stevenson replied, with slow, mocking anger.

There was no mistaking that tone of voice — he

thought *Brian* had left the bike out! "Oh, no! No way!" Brian said. He pointed to the exact place he'd left his bike in the garage. He remembered it, clear as day. "It was there! I parked it right there!"

"Right," Mr. Stevenson said. "So before I got into the car I placed it there myself. Forget it, Charlie. First my shirt, now this — what other traps have you set up for me? I'm already fifteen minutes late!"

"So what am I supposed to do about my bike? It's destroyed!"

Mr. Stevenson picked up the mangled bike with one hand. Brian felt a sharp pang of loss, as if he were looking at a pet that had just died. "Destroyed? Looks fine to me!" He dropped it beside the car and pointed to a tiny scratch on the rear bumper. "As it stands now, you're grounded for a week, no TV for the next seven nights, and you can consider yourself at the poverty level till this car is paid off!"

From the garage door, Brian's mom finally spoke up. "Don't you think that's a little rough?"

Mr. Stevenson wheeled around to her. "Don't make me the villain here, Holly."

"Wait!" Brian called out. "I'm out my bike — your bumper has a smudge on it. You run over *my* bike and *I* get punished?"

"Somebody had to put it here."

"Well, I didn't!"

Mr. Stevenson folded his arms and asked the

obvious question. The question that nailed Brian to the wall, because there was no way he could answer it for sure. "Then who did?"

Brian knew only these things: It wasn't his dad. It wasn't his mom. And it sure wasn't him.

There was only one other person who lived in the house. Only one other person who could possibly be guilty.

And right now, as far as Brian was concerned, no punishment was too harsh for his dear, innocent little brother.

Chapter 3

Eric shifted his lunch bag from one hand to the other. He was already getting tired of repeating his story to Todd.

"It didn't slime you?" Todd asked, for the second time. "You sure?"

"I think I'd know if I was slimed," Eric answered. "It just grabbed my ankle and whipped under my bed."

Todd furrowed his brow. As he walked along, he made sure to scuff his shiny new loafers in the dirt. Eric never understood why Todd's parents didn't let him wear sneakers to school. Then again, there were a lot of things Eric didn't understand about Todd. Like why he had to ask all these *questions*. Why couldn't he just take Eric's word for it?

"It didn't, like, go into the closet or look around for anything — you know, like come into your room for something?" Todd pressed.

"Nope."

Todd's blue eyes suddenly sparkled with hope.

"It didn't go by your desk and do your geography homework, did it?"

"Look, Todd," Eric said, raising his voice, "I never would have told you about it, but — "

"Okay . . . all right," Todd said, finally giving in. He ran his fingers through his dark hair, deep in thought. "So this is an exclusively under-the-bed phenomenon we're dealing with here."

"That's right. An exclusively under-the-bed phenomenon. Under *my* bed."

"Garlic!" Todd blurted out. "That's it! I read once that garlic keeps you safe from — "

"Vampires. It just works on vampires, Todd."

"Maybe if we pound a stake through its heart?" Todd shook his head at his own suggestion. "Nah, that's vampires, too."

"I think that'd work on anything," Eric replied.

"True . . . true. . . ."

As they turned the corner to the bus stop, Eric whispered, "Remember the promise, Todd. This is our secret."

The two of them fell silent and watched the bus pull up. As they climbed aboard and walked down the aisle, Eric tried to remember the names of some of the kids. After three weeks, he was finally beginning to recognize some faces.

Like the red-haired girl reading her science book, Kiersten Deveaux. Eric had to admit, she was pretty. Not that he liked girls or anything, but Kiersten was different from most girls. She always smiled and said hi, and didn't act snobby to kids who were new in school.

And she *liked* Brian. Eric could tell, just by the way she looked at him.

It made Eric want to laugh. Kiersten was a sixth-grader like Brian, and she was even in his class. So she probably gave him that look all the time. Eric would have *hated* that if he were Brian. It was easy being a third-grader, because you didn't have to worry about sixth-grade girls liking you. So it was okay if you liked them a *little*.

"Hi, Kiersten," he said. Of course, Todd had to say it at the same time, which was a little embarrassing.

She looked up with a friendly, open smile. "Hi."

Quickly Eric and Todd found a seat near the back of the bus just as it began to move.

A second later, the bus stopped short. Eric looked to the front and saw the door swing open. Bounding up the stairs, flushed from running, came Brian.

That's strange, Eric thought. Brian always said he hated the bus. He rode his bike to school every day.

Eric watched as Brian passed Kiersten. There was that *look* again. He was sure Brian would notice, but when Brian's eyes met hers, she looked away.

Brian walked right to the back of the bus and slipped into the seat behind Eric. "Eric," he said.

That was his way of saying hi. "Toad."

Eric could see his friend's face tighten slightly. Todd couldn't stand that nickname.

"Why aren't you riding your bike?" Eric asked.

"What bike?" Brian glared at him. "Dad ran over my bike because *you* left it in the driveway."

"No way!" Eric protested. He hated when Brian accused him of something he didn't do. "Your bike? No way!"

Their bodies lurched forward as the driver came to another bus stop. "I put it away," Brian said. "Mom and Dad sure didn't move it. That leaves *you*."

"I never touch your bike! I can hardly reach the pedals!"

But Brian wasn't buying the explanation. "That's it. You lie to me, you starve."

Before Eric could stop him, Brian grabbed his lunch bag and tossed it out the window.

"My lunch!" Eric shrieked. "You jerk! I didn't do anything!"

"Yeah?" Brian grabbed him by the shirt and brought his face inches away. "What about the ice cream? You snuck some ice cream last night, didn't you?"

"Forget it. Don't blame *that* on me!"

Eric had *had* it with these stupid accusations. He wasn't going to back down for one second. As he returned Brian's stare, he could tell his brother was softening.

Eric believed Brian, and now Brian seemed to believe Eric. The truth was, neither of them moved the bike, or put the ice cream in the cupboard. Which left a big question.

Who did?

"The monster," Todd said, with a confident nod.

Both Eric and Brian looked at him.

"That's it!" Eric replied. "That's what it was doing!"

Brian released his brother. With a smirk, he said to Todd, "He told you about the killer attack bunnies under his bed?"

"It was a monster," Eric insisted.

"There *are* no monsters," Brian said.

Their argument was cut off by a booming voice. "WHO'S ERIC?"

Brian, Eric, and Todd spun around.

Eric saw all nine years of his life pass before his eyes. Lumbering down the aisle, his face contorted with rage, was the last person any of them wanted to see.

Ronnie Coleman. Eric had never said the name aloud. *Thinking* it made him shudder. Behind Ronnie's demented eyes was a complex personality — the mind of a swamp rat, the body of an ape, and the personality of Godzilla. With a touch of Freddy Krueger thrown in. Rumor had it even his parents were afraid of him.

And there he was, grape juice splattered across his jersey, holding up a battered, dripping lunch bag.

A lunch bag with the name *ERIC* written on it in thick, black marker.

"Who's the 'Eric' who threw his lunch at me?" Ronnie roared.

Todd's panic-stricken eyes were the only things that moved. Right toward Eric.

Not now, you jerk! Eric wanted to scream.

Too late. Ronnie's murderous glare zeroed in on him. "You Eric?" he snarled.

Eric's neck muscles unfroze enough to permit a tiny nod.

"You want this back?" Ronnie asked.

Without waiting for an answer, Ronnie broke into a wide grin. Eric felt as if he'd been released from a torture chamber. He smiled with relief.

From the front of the bus came the driver's impatient voice: "Sit down back there!"

But Ronnie didn't. Instead he calmly opened Eric's lunch bag and pulled out the sandwich. Taking apart the slices of bread, he removed a limp, mustard-smeared piece of bologna. Then, as everyone watched, he dangled it in front of Eric.

That was enough for Brian. He shot up from his seat. "Hey!" he said, staring up at Ronnie. "Why don't you pick on someone your own size?"

"Yeah," Todd muttered, a little too loud, "like Big Foot."

A wave of shock collided with the fear that already hung in the air. With the bologna still in his hand, Ronnie bent his knees and lowered himself

. . . slowly . . . until he was finally eye-to-eye with Brian. "Maybe I will."

Out of the corner of Eric's eye, he could see Kiersten looking on with a mixture of disgust and admiration. It was easy to figure out which feeling went with whom.

SHREEEEEEEEEEE! Suddenly the driver slammed on the brakes. Eric and Todd flew forward against the seat in front of them. Brian grabbed onto a metal handle to keep his balance.

But there was nothing to stop Ronnie Coleman from reeling backward. He tumbled helplessly onto the floor, landing flat on his back with a dull thump.

On his jersey, resting on a sticky green-yellow coating of mustard, was Eric's slice of bologna.

A nervous giggle erupted from the front of the bus. One by one, the students began to laugh.

Turning around in anger, the bus driver shouted, "Get back to your seat or I'm locking up the windows and turning the heat on high!"

Slowly Ronnie rose from the floor. Anger radiated from him like a blast furnace. When he looked at Brian, his eyes blazed and his teeth clenched.

He only said four words to Brian, and he said them softly. But they were enough to make Brian's bones rattle.

"You're dead meat, Stevenson."

Chapter 4

"Fight . . . fight . . . fight!"

The chants echoed against the metal lockers in the school's hallway. Brian could see the crowd swelling around him. He backed away from Ronnie, who had changed into a clean baseball jersey. Inches away from Brian's face, Ronnie held out his mustard-splattered jersey.

"Stevenson," he said with a sadistic grin, "if it's the last thing I do today, I'm going to watch you eat my shirt."

"Coleman, I'm surprised you haven't eaten it already," Brian answered in a burst of bravery.

He felt his back making contact with a locker. There was no place to go. Ronnie's face was turning red with fury. His empty hand curled into a fist.

Brian did the only thing he could think of. He gave Ronnie a shove.

The crowd roared. Brian steeled himself for the fight of his life.

"Break it up!" came a loud voice. Brian's eyes

darted to the crowd. Pushing through it was the principal, Mr. Dutton. "Move out! Break it up!"

He clamped an arm on Brian and on Ronnie, pulling them apart. "*What* is going on here?"

"Sir," Ronnie replied, "I was just over here showing Brian what he did to my shirt, and he pushed me away."

"Oh, come on," Brian said.

Mr. Dutton threw Brian a harsh look. "Stevenson. You're new around here, aren't you?"

"Yes, sir."

"I think we're going to have a little talk — *in my office*." He grabbed Brian by the collar. "There are some rules to be learned around here."

Brian felt himself being pulled through the crowd and down the hallway. He was mortified. People he'd never met sure knew him now. Every pair of eyes was on him — curious, gleeful, mocking.

Or pitying. Like the look he was getting from Kiersten Deveaux.

The experiment was working. Here it was, the middle of the day, and the night-blooming cactus was actually in bloom!

Kiersten took a bite of her sandwich. Lunch period was the perfect time to work on a science project — nobody in the science room, no distractions.

She looked into a long wooden box. At one end was the cactus, at the other a bright light bulb. Two mirrors were on either side of the bulb. They reflected the light toward the middle of the box, where there was a prism. The prism turned the light into a rainbow of colors, which landed on the cactus.

Kiersten had been leaving the light on overnight and keeping the cactus in the dark during the day. Now she was getting results. She picked up a Polaroid camera from her desk and snapped a shot.

It clicked, but nothing came out. Kiersten reached into her pocket for her keys, then went over to a door marked FOR TEACHERS ONLY. Pulling out the key that Mr. Finn had given her, she smiled. No matter what anyone said, it really wasn't so bad being the teacher's pet.

She unlocked the door and yanked it open. "Light bulb city," she called this supply room. Over the years, Mr. Finn had collected lights the way some people collected books. Different shapes, different wattages — box after box stared down at her from the shelves. Stuffed around the edges were mechanical devices, switches, batteries, and boxes of film.

Kiersten grabbed some film, turned back to the classroom — and came face to face with Brian Stevenson.

"Oh!" she gasped.

"Wow!" Brian exclaimed, staring into the closet. "There's enough power in here to light up Yankee Stadium."

Kiersten quickly pulled herself together. "Already out on parole?" she remarked.

"Very funny." Brian peered around the classroom. "What's up, Miss *Deveaux*?"

26

If there was one thing Kiersten couldn't stand, it was when people pronounced her last name like Brian did — *DEE*-vo. It just went to show what a conceited creep he was. What did he think, that she was dying with passion for him or something?

Without answering, she slammed the closet door shut and dropped the film next to her camera.

As she turned to lock up, Brian lazily picked up the film and began loading the camera.

"You really want to know?" Kiersten asked coolly. "Or are you just asking?"

"I really want to know," Brian answered. He snapped the film in, faced the lens toward him, and held the camera at arm's length. The flashbulb went off as he snapped a shot of himself.

Kiersten snatched the camera out of his hands. "Disgusting — your face may corrode the camera!"

She walked away to the cactus box, half-hoping Brian would walk away — and half-hoping he wouldn't. Brian tossed the undeveloped photo on the table and followed her.

As she opened the box, Brian peered over her shoulder. "It's a night-blooming cactus," she explained. "I want to see if artificial sunlight changes its normal blooming pattern. I'm training it to bloom in the daytime." She smiled, admiring the prism and thinking about the magical colors it created. "Light is really fascinating. Who knows — I may be able to do something with it when I get older."

Immediately she wished she hadn't said that. Why was she letting herself open up to this gross guy? He wasn't going to understand. He'd probably make some sort of joke about it.

But Brian just nodded thoughtfully. "Helping humanity . . . that's nice. Your fellow humans . . . I like that."

Kiersten raised the camera and snapped the photo she'd been wanting to take. "To be scientific," she said, "I document the results with Polaroids."

Shutting the box, she threw the photo on a pile of other photos she'd been collecting over the weeks.

Brian picked up the picture and watched it develop. "Hey, you know what?" he asked excitedly.

Before she could stop him, he gathered up all her photos into a stack, sorting them into some kind of order. "If you mounted the camera in one place, upside down . . ." He turned the stack so that the white border faced up. "You could take a bunch of pictures and make it like a movie."

Holding the borders, he flipped through the stack. The cactus bloomed before Kiersten's eyes.

"Time-lapse photography!" she exclaimed. "That's great!"

Brian raised his eyebrows. "So I guess it's all set. We can team up on this project?"

For one moment — one moment only — she had begun to think this guy was all right. She should have suspected he was after something.

"Forget it, Brian," she said. "I'll end up doing all the work. No chance. Find someone else to leech off."

Brian's hands shot up into the air as he backed toward the door. "Take your time. Think about it. Maybe you'll change your mind."

With that, Brian slipped out of the room.

Good riddance, was Kiersten's first thought. The last thing she needed was some goon messing up her project.

Still, there was a strange, fluttery feeling inside her. Why was it she always seemed to have that feeling whenever she saw Brian? He definitely wasn't her type. Not someone who liked to pick fights, and was so in love with himself he had to take pictures of himself. Besides, who needed boys anyway? There were plenty of better things to spend your time with.

Kiersten vowed never to think of Brian again. She gathered up her project to put it away before the bell rang. But before throwing the photos in an envelope, she held them in front of her one more time. Carefully she grabbed the white borders and flipped through.

She smiled. It really *was* a good idea. Too bad someone like Brian had to think of it.

Chapter 5

Brian walked home, following the brick wall that lined the sidewalk. Great day, he thought gloomily.

One, his own father hated him.

Two, he'd made a mortal enemy of the most dangerous guy in school.

Three, the principal was convinced he was a hoodlum.

And four, he'd lost his chance for an easy passing grade in science.

Three strikes meant you were out. So what did four strikes mean?

Suddenly Brian heard footsteps behind him. They were running. It was more than one person — Ronnie and who else? For a moment, everything went blank. He had visions of going home with his features pummeled inside out.

"If you say there's no monster," a voice called out, "then switch rooms with me."

"What?" Brian spun around. He exhaled with relief. It was only Eric and Todd.

"Switch rooms with me," Eric repeated.

"Yeah," Todd added. "You sleep in Eric's room and he sleeps in your room."

Brian thought it over. He looked from one to the other. "You just want my room."

Immediately he knew he'd hit his mark — he could tell by the guilty looks on their faces. Turning his back, he continued walking down the street.

"Nuh-uh," came Eric's voice. He ran up alongside Brian. "I want you to prove me wrong. I *dare* you to switch rooms."

"Double dare him," Todd whispered into Eric's ear.

"Relax, Toad," Brian said.

But Eric barged right on. "I *double* dare you to switch rooms!"

Brian rolled his eyes. "Will you guys take a hike?"

"I'll pay you," Eric offered.

"I don't do pennies."

Eric dug into his pocket. "I've got . . . three dollars."

"And I have thirty-seven cents," Todd said, dumping change into Eric's hand. "That's — "

"I'll think about it," Brian interrupted, sparing Todd the addition problem.

Brian wasn't so sure this was the greatest idea — but hey, who couldn't use a little extra cash? Tightening his grip on the loaded basket he was carrying, he kicked the door open to Eric's room.

"You have to stay all night," Eric reminded him.

He ran in and grabbed his pajamas out of the closet. "*And* you have to sleep with your leg sticking out of the covers."

"And you have to keep the door closed," Todd piped up from behind Eric. His arms were wrapped around his Army/Navy sleeping bag, as if it were protecting him.

"Oh, stop, please," Brian said in a deadpan voice. "I can't take it. You're frightening me."

At that moment, Mr. Stevenson appeared in the doorway. "Eric, Todd — it's bedtime."

The two boys obediently walked out of the room and said a quick good night.

But Mr. Stevenson lingered at the door. He's probably going to yell at me again, Brian thought. Or give me some crazy punishment I don't deserve.

He turned to the bed and pulled Eric's covers down, trying to look busy.

"Brian," his dad said, "I came in here to tell you how proud I am of you for switching rooms with Eric."

What? *Proud?* Brian felt himself perk up. That was the first nice thing his dad had said all day. He turned to face him.

"Actually," Mr. Stevenson continued, "I think you're both crazy and if you see any monsters tonight, make sure to get some autographs for me."

They both laughed. "Okay, Dad," Brian said. "See you in the morning . . . if I make it."

"Right. Good night!"

Brian hopped into bed and immediately started

to fall asleep. He was aware of a voice in his dream — a low, whispering voice, somehow very familiar. A voice trying hard to be scary, but not really making it. . . .

Brian's eyes popped open. It was Todd's voice, telling a ghost story. And it wasn't a dream. The voice was drifting down from the attic.

He flipped around and tried to get back to sleep, but it was impossible.

"So . . . um, so the girl's waiting for her roommate to get back," Todd's voice continued, "and she's getting real scared . . . oh, yeah, the room's on the second floor. . . ."

Todd's story-telling was *terrible*! Brian felt himself cringe with every sentence.

"So she's waiting, and it's probably the darkest night ever. *Suddenly*, from outside, she hears 'thump-THUMP . . . thump-THUMP,' so she gets real brave and inches her way to the door. And she hears it again: 'thump-THUMP . . . thump-THUMP'!"

Enough was enough. Brian threw the bedcovers to the floor and hopped out of bed. He grabbed a hockey stick that was leaning against the wall and quietly left the room.

As he tiptoed his way up the stairs, Todd's voice got clearer. "So this girl is standing by the door and the 'thump-THUMP' is getting louder and louder. . . ."

Brian poised himself on the stairs, just below the attic. He gripped the butt of the hockey stick. Come on, Todd, he thought. Get to the good part. It'll be a lot scarier than you ever imagined!

"She opens the door and screams — but nothing will come out," Todd continued. "She looks out, terrified, as her roommate comes up the stairs — only the ax-man cut off all her arms and legs, and she's dragging herself up by her chin . . . 'thump-THUMP . . . thump-THUMP . . . thump-THUMP.' " He paused. "Pretty incredible, huh?"

"It really happened?" Eric asked.

"I'm deadly serious, man," Todd replied. "My brother Freddie told me it happened to a friend of a friend of a distant cousin of a cousin of ours."

Grinning evilly, Brian pounded the hockey stick against the stairs: thump-THUMP . . . thump-THUMP . . . thump-THUMP. . . .

Todd and Eric stopped talking. Brian could practically see them shaking in their pajamas. He raced down the stairs, fighting the urge to laugh out loud.

He burst through the door to Eric's room — and stopped in his tracks.

A strange, grayish-blue glow filled the room. It poured out of the sides of the closet, along with the hollow *hisssss* of static. On Eric's bed, the bedcovers had been bunched up in a pile against the wall. Brian could have sworn he'd thrown them on the floor before he left.

Brian flipped up the light switch, but nothing happened.

Slowly he approached the closet door. The static

noise grew louder. He wrapped his hand around the knob and pulled.

His mouth fell open. There, sitting on its side on the closet floor, was the family TV set.

This had to be a trick, Brian told himself — Eric must have put it there earlier. Right now the most important thing was not to let his parents hear it. He reached down to the on/off button.

Suddenly he yanked his hand back. Before his eyes, the channels began changing. Talk shows, movies, commercials flicked on and off the screen.

WHACK!

Brian felt his whole body jump at the slamming noise behind him. He whipped around.

Like a whirling top, the remote controller came spinning out from under the bed. Brian gaped at it in awe.

What was going on here?

He glanced back to the TV. But when his eyes returned to the floor, the remote controller was slowly sliding back under the bed.

Brian knelt down. He peered into the shadow beneath the bed. The dull light from the TV was enough to illuminate the area. Enough to show that there was nothing there.

The remote controller had disappeared.

Brian sprang back from the bed. He felt beads of warm sweat on his forehead.

There was only one explanation, he realized. *Eric was right!*

Chapter 6

The next morning, Eric and Todd stood over Brian's sleeping figure on the living room sofa. Mr. and Mrs. Stevenson had been painting the night before, and the strong smell of fresh enamel drifted through the room. Despite that, Brian slept soundly, covered with a paint-spattered drop cloth.

Eric grinned with delight. "I wish I had a camera. Look at him."

"Three dollars and thirty-seven cents," Todd said. "We're rich."

In the corner a grandfather clock chimed. Brian shifted positions.

"Hey, Brian!" Eric called out. "You okay?"

Brian just lay there, his eyes shut tightly.

"Looks like you got *two* weird phenomenons in your house," Todd remarked. "A monster and a giant chicken."

Even the insult brought no response from Brian.

"Maybe the monster's got his tongue," Eric said.

Todd smirked. "He doesn't need a tongue to pay up."

That did it. Brian's sleepy voice arose from the sofa. "Double or nothing."

The look in Todd's eyes expressed exactly what Eric was feeling. His brother must have gone crazy.

Brian wiped the sweat off his brow and looked at his creation. It was perfect. A foolproof monster trap — and he'd gotten all the parts he needed right out of the garage. In fact, now he was *glad* his bike had been mangled. He hadn't felt guilty taking it apart.

He cranked the pedal, which moved the chain, which turned the rear sprocket. It worked the same way the bike did — except the sprocket was attached to a rope instead of the rear wheel. Brian had tied the other end of the rope to the bed — and had suspended the middle section of the rope from a pulley on the ceiling.

As Brian cranked, the rope pulled taut. He squeezed the brake handle and wrapped a rubber band around it. That held the brake pads in place, gripped firmly onto the wheel. If the grip was strong enough, the rope wouldn't move.

Then he reached under the bed. He had unscrewed the legs, leaving the bed to be supported only by a few stacks of books. Now he pulled the books away.

The bed remained up, suspended over the floor. Brian stepped back and looked at his creation.

Obviously *something* was living under the bed. All Brian had to do was wait until it came out, then slam the bed down on the floor. The monster would be stranded!

With a triumphant smile, Brian eased into bed and waited.

It wasn't long before his mom popped into the room. Her face, hands, and clothes were speckled with paint. She placed a flashlight on the night-stand. "Eric wanted you to have this."

Brian gave her a long look. With a sinking feeling in his stomach, he realized it might be the last time he saw her. Who knew what the monster would do to him?

"Brian? Are you feeling okay?" she asked.

"Fine, Ma. Never felt better."

"Then what are you doing in bed at nine-fifteen?"

"School, Ma. Big day ahead of me. Big, big day!"

She kissed him on the forehead. "It sounds nice, Brian, but I'm not sure I believe it."

Brian flashed a grin. "It's the new me."

"Well," his mom said, surveying the room, "the new you better clean up this old mess by tomorrow." She turned to leave.

Brian felt a pang. He didn't want her to leave — not on those words. He had to say something. "I . . . I love you."

She smiled. "I love you, too, honey." With that, she walked away, closing the door behind her.

Brian listened to her footsteps recede down the hallway. When he couldn't hear them anymore, he jumped out of bed and turned on the light. He pulled the covers off the bed, revealing the monster-hunting gear he'd stored underneath: scissors, an alarm clock, a spool of heavy-duty fishing line, the hockey stick, and a big bag of Doritos.

Working fast, he tied one end of the fishing line to the bell-striker of the alarm clock, then crisscrossed the line all around the room. Next, he removed the knob from the inside of the door. If Brian happened to fall asleep, the monster would trip the wire and set off the alarm bell. And if it tried to escape, it wouldn't be able to open the door.

With monsters, you couldn't take any chances.

Brian lay down on the bed again, placing the flashlight on the pile next to him along with the hockey stick and the scissors.

He made a few quick practice grabs. Each time, his fingers clutched precisely around the scissors.

He was ready.

Two hours later, he was still ready. And bored. And hungry. As moonlight filtered through the window, he munched on some Doritos — moving his jaw slowly, quietly. . . .

Just then he had an idea. Monsters must get hungry, too. If this monster wasn't going to come out, maybe Brian could lure it out.

He leaned over and scattered Doritos on the floor around the bed. With a tingle of excitement, he stretched out and waited.

* * *

Brian shifted in and out of consciousness. He wondered how long it took for Doritos to become stale. Definitely by three hours! That was how long ago he'd put them down.

But maybe monsters liked them stale. Maybe . . . maybe. . . .

Brian wasn't thinking straight. Dream shapes began to form in his mind. Maybe the monster would come tomorrow night. . . .

Crunch.

Brian's eyes snapped open.

Crunch. Crunch.

He pulled the blanket around him tighter.

Crunch.

Slowly he turned his eyes toward the center of the room. The crunching stopped.

Brian felt his muscles freeze. All he could see was the gaping blackness of the bedroom.

And that's when the chomping started again. The unmistakable sound of someone — some*thing* — munching on Doritos.

Brian's fingers quivered as he closed them around the scissors. With his other hand, he groped for the hand brake, touching the rubber band. He felt his lungs screaming for him to take a breath — but he couldn't. Not yet.

RRRRRRINNNNNNNNG!

The alarm! The monster was in the room! With a swift, sure motion, Brian cut the rubber band. The brake pads opened. The wheel turned. The sprocket spun. The rope released.

With a deafening crash, the bed collapsed to the floor.

Brian flicked his flashlight on and spun toward the center of the room.

The edge of the beam caught something rushing toward the bed. Brian caught a glimpse of eerie-looking eyes. Before he could train the light on it, it hurtled back into the darkness.

Frantically Brian passed the light back and forth across the room. The shrill ringing of the alarm clock began to quiet down.

In seconds there was nothing but silence. The light beam traced out only the image of Eric's messy room — books, tapes, clothing, and sports equipment on the floor.

Brian's shoulders slumped. He peered into the darkness. Could it have been a dream?

No. The Doritos were crushed, or missing. And the door was still closed. That meant the monster *had* to be in the room.

Somewhere.

Whap! Brian screamed as an arm slapped across his chest. He jerked his body forward, and whatever attacked him went tumbling over his shoulder.

It thudded to the floor, and Brian pounced. His flashlight had fallen to the floor, but there was no time to look for it. Brian wrestled with his unseen enemy, rolling around, thrashing with his arms. He felt himself hurtle through the air and crash against a wall.

He straightened up into a wrestling stance. In

the darkness, he could make out a large form flying toward him. He jumped on it, threw it down, pinned it. Victory at last! With one hand he felt around furiously for the flashlight. . . .

Click.

Suddenly the room was flooded with light. Brian shielded his eyes. He squinted toward the doorway to see a tall, familiar silhouette.

"Dad!" he screamed. "The monst — "

But something felt wrong. Brian looked down at his victim.

His eyes grew wide. Beneath his legs was a pile of clothes — a T-shirt, jeans, sneakers, and a black leather vest with lots of pins and buttons on it.

No monster.

Unless, of course, you counted Mr. Stevenson, whose shocked, angry face was beginning to look more and more like a fright mask.

Chapter 7

Mr. Stevenson's bloodshot eyes scanned the room. "What on earth is this? Look at this mess! It looks like four tornados hit." He stepped inside.

Crunch.

"And what are these?" He looked under his slipper. "*Doritos?* On the floor?"

"I'll clean them up," Brian hastily said.

Mr. Stevenson was fuming. "Don't bother — you'll need the nutrition. Starting in the morning, your door is locked till this room is clean!"

"Wait a minute!" Brian protested. "There is a monster. You have to believe me!"

"A monster? Brian, you are wrestling a pile of clothes, for heaven's sake!"

He kicked at the T-shirt, which swept limply to one side. With an exasperated look, he turned to leave.

Snap!

Almost too fast to see, one of the T-shirt sleeves flicked his dad's ankle.

Pile of clothes, huh? Brian thought. He couldn't help but smile.

Mr. Stevenson turned around, bewildered. He looked at the clothes, then at Brian. "What are you smiling for? After you finish with this room, I'll expect to see you outside pushing a lawn mower." Storming out of the room, he grabbed behind him to close the door.

No! Brian wanted to warn him. *Don't touch the doorknob!*

Too late. It came off in his hand.

Now the veins in his neck were beginning to bulge. If a volcano could speak, it would have sounded like Mr. Stevenson's hissing voice: "And after the hedges are cut, you'll be in the garage, cleaning it out!"

He snapped the light off and stepped into the hallway, slamming the door behind him.

The last thing Brian saw before the light went out was his flashlight. He dove for it. Grasping it, he sprang to his feet and trained the beam on the pile of clothes. With his free hand, he reached for the hockey stick.

Cautiously he jabbed the stick into the clothes.

Once.

Twice.

There was no response. He inched closer and gave them a good poke.

Whack! The sleeve knocked the hockey stick out

of Brian's hand. He jumped back in fright, losing his grip on the flashlight.

As it clattered to the floor, Brian felt panic shoot through him like a sharp winter wind.

And before his eyes, the clothes began to gather into themselves — whirling, twitching furiously until they took on a hunched, human shape.

Brian grabbed for the nearest object — a wicker laundry basket. He slammed it down over the clothes and threw himself on top. The motion stopped. The clothes were trapped.

Brian sighed with relief. His thoughts raced around in his head. Obviously the monster had a weakness — light. It thrived in the darkness, but when the light was on, it turned into a pile of clothes. Now, if only he could find the flashlight. . . .

WHAAAAM! The basket exploded, hurling Brian into the air. A scream welled up in his throat, but it didn't have time to escape. Flailing helplessly, Brian smashed against the wall.

He slid down and bounced gently onto the bed. He tried to focus his eyes. A large figure was standing over him — or was it two? Images split and then came together in front of Brian. His mind reeled with the pain. He blinked several times, until his vision was crowded by one figure.

Brian swallowed. It was beyond ugly. It made Ronnie Coleman look like Tom Cruise. Between its gnarled, deformed ears was a pasty purplish face covered with dark blotches. A sparse field of colorless hair stuck out the top of its head, like hay that hadn't been cut. Underneath a black leather jacket with cut-off sleeves, its clothes were ripped and dirty.

I'm dead, Brian thought. They'll come in here tomorrow, find me mangled on the floor, and call it the unsolved mystery of the century. They'll make a TV movie about it. Mom and Dad will get rich from it, and they'll spend all the money on Eric.

The monster stared at Brian without expression. Then it lifted its right arm waist-high.

Brian flinched and turned away. But when he looked back, the arm was still extended, fingers toward him.

It wants to shake my hand, Brian realized. He glanced around, looking for a way to escape. But he was cornered. The smartest thing he could do was give in. He reached out to grab the monster's hand.

But just before their fingers touched, the monster yanked its hand away.

Its face broke into a wide grin, revealing a row of jagged teeth. Brian didn't know whether to smile or get sick.

As if to answer Brian's dilemma, the monster's eyes shot out of their sockets toward him.

Brian choked back a scream. Losing his balance, he tumbled off the bed and onto a throw rug. He backed away and grabbed the rug, giving it a solid yank. The monster's feet went out from underneath it. With a whomp, it landed hard on its back.

Brian leaped over the monster and ran to the door. He reached out to open it.

Horror sliced through him as his hand brushed against the metal stump where he had removed the knob.

There was only one option left — the window. Brian ran toward it and took a flying leap.

In midair, the fishing line wrapped around Brian's ankle and pulled tight. He dropped to the floor and looked up.

Grinning, the monster reeled him in. Brian swiped at the line with his hands. He tried to tear it away, all the time sliding closer and closer to the monster's misshapen hands. Then, with a strength he didn't know he had, he pulled his leg free. Rolling away, he grabbed the hockey stick.

The monster looked forlornly at the end of the broken fishing line. It lifted the line up to see the alarm clock attached to the other end. Furrowing its brow, it looked at the time.

Instantly it dropped the clock and ran for the bed.

Oh, no you don't! Brian thought. He jumped between the monster and the bed, lifting his hockey stick high. The monster stopped short.

For a long moment, the two of them stared at each other. Then, with a snarl, the monster raised its hands. Sharp claws extended from its knobby fingers.

"I'll scream," Brian threatened.

For the first time, the monster spoke. "Go right ahead. And this time your dad'll bust in here and ground you for life." It flashed a sly grin. "Actually, maybe *I'll* scream."

It stepped back and took a deep breath. Brian's eyes glazed with anger. He had had enough. Jumping across the room, he socked the monster in the stomach.

"Shut up," Brian snarled angrily.

The monster raised a hand and backed away, gasping. "Whoa, time out! What's your dad going to say when he sees Dorito-puke all over the floor?"

Brian stood back, watching the monster stagger across the room, inching closer and closer to the bed. . . .

In one quick motion, Brian picked a book off the floor and threw it. The monster ducked, and the book sailed across the room to a window on the opposite wall.

With a clatter, the blind flew open. Early-morning light blanketed the room.

The monster's knees buckled. It cast a wide-eyed glance at the window, its evil expression turning to panic.

Brian smiled. This couldn't have worked better if he'd planned it. He stepped in front of the bed, gazing out into the silvery dawn. "Why don't we just watch the sun rise?"

The monster grimaced with a sudden, sharp pain. Just above its ears, two small horns burst their way through the skin. Shrieking, the monster clasped its head.

"Great," it said bitterly. "Like I really needed two horns, badly. No one's going to recognize me."

Before Brian could respond, the monster threw a body block at him. He fell backward as the monster dove for the bed and dug its fingers under the mattress.

It pulled up with its hands — and its fingers passed right through. The mattress didn't budge.

The monster stared at its hands, horrified.

Brian leaped onto the mattress. He lowered the hockey stick in front of the bed, prying the monster away. Reaching desperately, the monster fell to the floor. Its feet had begun to shrivel.

Slowly the monster's skin began to sizzle, sending up wisps of smoke.

"What's happening?" Brian asked, astonished.

"Bacon and eggs, kid," the monster answered. "Sunny-side up or over easy?"

"You're dying!" Now Brian understood it all. "The sunlight — first it disfigures you, then it kills you. And regular indoor light turns you into clothes."

"Puh-leeze!" the monster said, its voice raspy and choked. "I have to get back under the bed before the sun totally rises."

"No way! You wrecked my bike. You've been

pulling stuff, trying to get me in trouble."

"That's my *job!*" the monster croaked. "I get kids in trouble!"

The monster cringed on the floor, its skin melting as the rays of the rising sun grew ever stronger. It looked at Brian with wide, pleading eyes. Gone was the mischief, the terrifying sneer. In its place was the helpless look of a child in pain.

Brian felt his arms go limp. He watched the monster's eyelids droop closed. Its body had become a hissing heap on the floor.

"Terrific," he muttered gloomily. Somehow, this wasn't what he'd expected. Instead of enjoying his victory, he felt hollow and sad.

With both hands, he lifted up the corner of the bed. He looked tentatively at the monster.

Slowly its eyes flickered open. With every last ounce of strength, it tried to pull itself toward the bed. But it was no use. Its arms and legs had shriveled.

With a sigh, Brian reached down and wrapped his arms around the monster's torso. Straining to hold the mattress up with one hand, he dragged it into the shadow underneath.

The monster disappeared into the dark world, and Brian let the mattress drop. He collapsed to the floor, exhausted.

He barely had time to catch his breath when the bed began to move. It rose slowly off the floor, as if it were on a hydraulic lift. Brian jumped away.

Out of the inky darkness below, the monster

emerged, holding the bed over its head with one hand. It was completely back to normal — if "normal" was what you could call it — and a wide smile lit up its face.

With a gleeful whisper, it said, "The name's Maurice, and I'll catch you later."

And it was the last thing the monster said before disappearing into the shadow again.

Chapter 8

This was *not* the way Brian liked to spend his holidays. Tired enough to collapse, cleaning junk out of the garage, and having to deal with Eric tagging along behind him. *After* having spent the early hours raking the lawn!

He carried a bulging plastic trash bag to the front of the house. Lined up neatly in the gutter were all the other trash bags he'd filled — with leaves, kitchen garbage, and junk from the garage. With a grunt, he dropped the bag next to the others. It clanked dully on the asphalt. This one was full of all Mr. Stevenson's old unwanted gadgets — except for one. As Brian turned to trudge back up the driveway, Eric peppered him with questions.

"You're telling me there are no monsters?"

"Not after last night," Brian answered. He walked into the garage and looked around. It was almost neat, he realized with relief. But there was still one important task to do. He picked up an old Super-8 movie projector, the one thing he'd rescued from his dad's pile of junk. Now it belonged with Brian's new collection — a collection of lights he had begun to hoard against a back wall. He dropped it gently into the pile.

It all might be useful someday.

Brian began cleaning up the remaining mess in the garage. "So," he continued. "I'll be taking my master suite back."

"Then what was that rumble I heard down there last night?" Eric persisted.

"Rumble? That was a nuclear war! It's not easy defeating the Army, Navy, Air Force, and Marines all wrapped up in a single creature uglier than you!"

"Yeah, right," Eric said skeptically.

"Would I lie to you?"

The sound of their parents' voices cut off their conversation. When Brian had left the house, their mom had been sanding down the living-room wall while their dad was shaving upstairs. Now they were together and bickering again, loud enough to be heard outside.

"Where's the remote controller?" Mr. Stevenson's voice boomed. "How is a human being supposed to watch TV without remote control? *Brian* must know!"

As Brian put the last garden tool away, he heard the back window of the house being flung open.

"Brian . . . Eric!" came Mr. Stevenson's voice. "The Celts are on, the Sox are on, and so is the Masters, and I'm without a remote controller. Where is it?"

The brothers emerged from the garage. Staring blankly at their father, they shrugged.

Just then Brian heard a clanking noise from the street. He tore off, running up the driveway to the front of the house.

When he got there, he stopped short. His morning's work was now chaos. Everything he'd so carefully stuffed in the trash bags was now scattered all over the street, the sidewalk, and the front lawn. His eyes darted left toward a figure that was receding down the street.

A figure pedaling furiously on a bicycle, with the name COLEMAN stitched onto the back of his shirt.

"EEEEEAAAAAAGHHHH!"

Brian sat up in bed at the sound of Eric's scream. The monster had lived up to its promise and returned the next night.

Unfortunately for Eric, it had returned to *his* room, expecting to find Brian there.

Brian scrambled out of bed. The monster would probably realize in an instant that the brothers had switched rooms — and this time, Brian was *really* prepared for a visit. No more dinky little flashlight. This monster was going to walk into a light show!

The moon shone dimly through the window as Brian groped for the switch he had rigged.

He recoiled when a small metal object flew up from the floor and hit him in the face. As it dropped to the floor, Brian saw that it was the remote controller his dad had been looking for. Raucous, out-of-tune singing wafted into the room from under his bed.

Brian cautiously poised his finger on the light switch and held his breath.

Out of nowhere, Maurice appeared. His annoyed face was silhouetted in the soft moonlight. "Why'd you switch rooms with that Wiffle Ball? He's going to have a heart attack before he's ten."

Now! Brian said to himself. He flipped the switch. From every corner of the room, a light glared — the overhead light, two tall floor lamps without shades, a mechanic's light, the Super-8 movie lamp, and a string of blinking miniature Christmas lights. A jumble of extension cords stretched across the floor, connecting them all together.

Instantly Maurice disappeared. In his place was the same pile of clothes Brian had wrestled to the floor the night before.

"Surprise!" Brian said jubilantly.

His smile vanished when the pile of clothes began to speak. "Brilliant, Bri. Just brilliant. I love it. Now, how about lighting a candle? These lights are painful, man!"

"Forget it. I've got enough problems without you running around getting me into trouble."

"You got your stupid remote controller back. Turn off the lights."

Maurice was right about the remote controller, but there was something strange about it. It felt lighter than usual — and there was only one explanation for that.

"What about the batteries?" Brian demanded.

"I ate them for breakfast," Maurice answered, with an angry edge to his voice.

"What about my bike?"

"I'll get you a new bike." Maurice raised his voice with a shout. *"Just get me out of these clothes!"*

"Sssshhhhhh!" Brian waved his arms, hoping his parents hadn't heard.

"Honest, I'm burning up. My seams are on fire."

Brian knew he had the upper hand. And by the tone of Maurice's voice, Maurice knew it, too. With renewed confidence, Brian picked up the flashlight off the floor. "All right," he said, "but any funny moves and you're clothes!"

He flicked the light switch. There was a sudden spark from one of the extension cords. The room plunged into darkness, except for the Christmas lights, which Brian had connected separately — as a precaution.

As Maurice materialized into his old self, the lights cast a dancing pattern of colors on his face. Brian realized that *some* light — like the moon and the Christmas lights — were too weak to affect Maurice.

"Grazie, grazie!" Maurice said, using the Italian word for thank you. "You know, you're a pretty sharp kid. Ugly, but sharp. I've been in this business for over two hundred years and never been trapped once."

"How old are you?" Brian asked.

"Eleven." Maurice glanced at his dim reflection in Brian's wall mirror. "And I am not getting any prettier."

Then, as Brian looked on in disgust, Maurice picked a round, black mole off his face and tossed it at him.

Brian ducked away. "How could you be eleven?"

"Hey, where I live, you don't age," Maurice said. He walked over to the bed. "You don't realize it, but today is your lucky day!"

"What do you mean?" Brian asked with an eager grin. "Like I get three wishes?"

"*Wishes?*" Maurice glared at him scornfully. "Wishes are strictly bush-league leprechaun, pal. I'm a monster. Monsters don't do wishes."

"Then what do you do?"

Without the slightest effort, Maurice lifted the bed on its end. "I have the time of my life!" He gave Brian a welcoming smile. "Come down, take a look for yourself."

He lifted his foot, then placed it down under the bed. It sank down beyond the floor and into the shadow.

"How'd you do that?" Brian asked. He reached his hand into the shadow.

It stubbed against the floor.

"Magic, chump," Maurice said. "You have to be handsome and gorgeous like me — or have someone as handsome and gorgeous as me to help you. What do you say?" His voice broke into an imitation of a game-show host: "Come on dooowwwwn!"

Brian stared blankly. He felt gripped with uncertainty. "I can't."

"What are you talking about, 'you can't'? Ooooh, I hate that word. You can't jam a basketball, you can't get hit by a grenade and survive — *those* things you can't do. But you *can* take a walk on the wild side."

Brian jumped back, clutching the flashlight. "And how do I know if I go down there, I'll be able to return?"

Maurice's features drooped into a puppylike stare. "Does this look like a face you can't trust?"

Brian couldn't help chuckling. But his mind was made up. "Forget it. If my parents find out I'm sneaking around in the middle of the night, they'll kill me. . . . Actually first they'll have me clean every square inch of the house, and *then* they'll kill me."

"Brian, listen to me. What goes on down there is every kid's fantasy. Imagine a world solely of kids. Kids that just want to have fun — "

"And make trouble," Brian interrupted.

"Trouble is our code of honor — our blood, our life-support system! *Blame!* Without us there'd be no such word in the English language!"

"Do they all look like you?"

"Only the good-looking ones," Maurice answered without missing a beat. "Think of it, Brian. No teachers, no rules, no homework, no parents. Did you hear me, boy? I said *no parents!* Man, that alone

58

is worth all the money in the world!"

He let it sink in. Brian began imagining Maurice's world — and it didn't seem so bad.

"Brian, it's about leaving your clothes where you want to leave them. It's about not cleaning up after you eat. It's about never having to be on time. It's about staying up late and watching whatever it is you feel like watching — David Letterman, *anything*. It's about nailing someone who bugs you in a way you never dreamed possible. It's about total, unadulterated, one-hundred-percent, solid-state, where's-the-beef anarchy!"

Brian felt himself bristling with excitement. Maurice leaned closer to him. "It's about freedom, Bri. Freedom to live life like the creators of this planet intended it."

His words hung in the air like a chord after the finish of a song.

When Brian spoke, his voice was a humble whisper. "Man, that sounds good."

Maurice reached out to him, beckoning toward the shadow. "What do you say? You ready?"

Thoughts careened in Brian's head. Half of him wanted to flick on the lights and run away. He imagined the look on his parents' faces if they found him gone. He saw Eric growing up confused, without an older brother to bug. But still . . . *no rules* . . . there was a feeling inside him more powerful than he'd ever imagined. Maybe Maurice *was* trustworthy. After all, he owed Brian one. . . .

Finally Brian looked up, his eyes burning with

intensity. "Maurice," he said in measured tones. "I was born ready."

Maurice wasted no time. He grabbed Brian's arm and pulled.

Brian dropped the flashlight. "Wait a minute!" he said, scooping it up. "I need some insurance."

"Whoa there, Thunder!" Maurice shook his head. "Matches, candles, even a torch — but definitely *no* lights!"

Brian pointed the flashlight upward and flipped on the switch. He angled it menacingly toward Maurice.

"All right, all right!" Maurice cried. "But I'm telling you, you'd better keep it hidden."

There was nothing holding Brian back now. He had a weapon. Stuffing the flashlight into his pocket, he allowed Maurice to pull him toward the bed.

He stepped into the shadow, bracing his foot for contact with the floor.

But there was no floor. Or if there was, Brian had just stepped through it.

Screaming, he plunged into darkness. And the last thing he saw of his room was the bed dropping down onto its legs above him.

Chapter 9

Brian landed in a heap on a dark floor. Beside him was a set of stairs leading upward. Why didn't Maurice *tell* me about that? he thought, wincing with pain.

He looked up to see Maurice sailing down through the darkness. After a graceful half gainer, he landed on his feet beside Brian. With a friendly smile, he reached down to help Brian up.

And suddenly Brian began to see the world around him.

It was almost as if a light had gone on. But it wasn't a light. Brian could tell this place was dark — and yet he could see everything.

"What the — ?" he whispered.

As if reading his mind, Maurice said, "Hey, when you sleep your eyes are closed — and yet your dreams are all lit up, right? Think about it. This is the same kind of light — not that crude *bulb* stuff you have in the so-called real world!" He gestured around him. "Only difference is, *this* ain't no dream, pal!"

Brian's jaw hung open. Bathed in the eerie glow, the netherworld stretched out in all directions — around him, below him, above him. There was no floor, no ceiling. Just levels and levels of catwalks, archways, walls, rope bridges, terraces — all suspended in midair, all connected to each other with ladders, stairs, ropes, and poles.

Chutes and Ladders, Brian thought. The place was like one huge Chutes and Ladders game. A barely audible "Wow" was all he could muster.

Maurice was already bounding down a nearby companionway. He turned to see Brian gaping. "Yo! Brian!" he called out. "Let's move 'em out! We're burning night-light, pard!"

Brian started after him, still gazing around him in awe. "What's with all these stairs?"

Maurice led him past a forked hallway. To the left was a sign that read LOS ANGELES, to the right a sign reading NEW YORK. "Friend," he said, "every one of those leads to some poor soul's bedroom, a veritable cornucopia of mischief! Let me show you around before we do some business."

Suddenly Brian was following Maurice into an enormous room that practically exploded with noise.

Brian's pulse raced. Heaven, he thought. I have entered heaven itself. There was nothing in the room but arcades. They overlapped one another, ringing with the sound of pinball machines, video games, air hockey, and foosball. Music blared from racks of stereo systems and jukeboxes. In the middle of it all was a gargantuan bin of quarters labeled MOM'S CHANGE.

A compact disc sliced through the air. Brian followed it with his eyes. It was caught by the most hideous creature he'd ever seen. In fact, everyone in the room — every *thing* that crowded around the machines — was more bizarre-looking than the one next to it. All of them were short, all of them kids. There were monsters that looked like animals, monsters that looked like deformed dolls, monsters that would have scared Brian out of his mind if he'd seen them any other time but now.

But somehow it didn't seem to matter. What mattered was digging into MOM'S CHANGE and getting to one of those pinball machines — as soon as possible!

As Brian whacked the flippers, Maurice watched with a tolerant smile. The all-time highest score glowed at the top of the screen: 12,973,639. Brian couldn't believe *anyone* ever got that high. His score was *millions* lower than that and he was on his fourth ball. As the ball rolled agonizingly down between the flippers, he twisted his body right and left, as if that would change the ball's course.

Suddenly, an instant before the ball disappeared, Maurice picked the machine up. The ball rolled back to the top.

"Hey, what are you doing?" Brian demanded. "You'll tilt it!"

Maurice shoved Brian aside and took over the

controls. "Bri, baby — open your eyes, honey, kid! Down here there's no such thing as tilt!"

He was right. The ball ricocheted wildly as he bumped and shoved the machine. Brian watched the score climb, then glanced around him. It was incredible — unlimited machines, unlimited games, no tilt, *no rules.*

Brian was beginning to think he could live here the rest of his life.

Next stop was the dining room — at least that's what Maurice called it. To Brian, it was even more perfect than the game room. There were pool tables, not dinner tables. And Brian's mouth watered at the collection of food heaped on each one.

Burgers, hot dogs, bottles of ketchup, mustard, and relish. Soda, cookies, snack packs, chocolate bars, cereals, Pop Tarts, Kool-Aid. And ice cream — cartons and cartons and cartons, every flavor he could think of. As monsters devoured the food, boxes and scraps flew in the air.

If all dining rooms in the United States were like this, Brian thought, kids would never, ever have any trouble eating.

Maurice and Brian dove in, eating whatever they could get their hands on. As Maurice munched on a hot dog, he gave Brian a proud look. "It's my favorite spot on the planet. Every craving you've ever craved, every flavor you've ever flaved. Do you see any parents here telling kids what not to eat? Do you?"

"No," Brian said, tossing a fried-chicken bone over his shoulder.

Maurice stuffed a cake under his vest. "For later," he said.

Without any warning, everyone stopped eating. There was a split second of silence as they all took a deep breath. Then, like a rumbling of thunder, one huge belch erupted. Brian doubled over laughing.

All at once, everyone left the room. Maurice grabbed Brian and ran after them.

"Who cleans up?" Brian asked, looking at the chaos behind them.

"Cleans?" Maurice repeated. "What is there in here that needs cleaning?"

Passing them in the opposite direction were three monsters carrying large metal canisters. Brian looked over his shoulder and watched them point the canisters at the room.

With a deafening roar, flames shot out. Fire raged through the room, but only briefly.

When it was over, the mess was gone.

Maurice led Brian to a long counter — the "assignment area." Brian had been one of Maurice's assignments this week, and now it was time for some new ones.

The attendant lifted his gnarled face to Maurice. "Who's the drip?"

Brian bristled at the insult. But before he could respond, Maurice said, "Ease off, Schmoog. He saved me from a fatal case of sunburn, so I'm giving him the grand tour."

Schmoog shrugged. "Oh." He reached behind him, pulled three cards out of a mail slot, and tossed them on the counter. "You got an imp in Atlanta, a brat in Cleveland, and a twerp in Boston. Go out there tonight and make us proud!"

Maurice grabbed the cards. Brian followed him away from the table, bewildered. "Wait a minute. Don't tell me you have an airport down here?"

"Brian, look around," Maurice answered. "Does any one of these hunchbacks look like he could handle a plane? It's magic!" He pointed to a signpost that looked like it had been stolen from a city street up in the real world. To the right, the sign pointed to Tokyo, Sydney, Paris, London, and Berlin. To the left it pointed to Appleton, Wisconsin. "Down here distance is like magic."

Maurice was cut off by a flying body and a loud thud. The signpost wobbled. Beneath it, a short monster lay crumpled where he had smacked into it.

Behind Maurice and Brian, there was a sound of thundering footsteps. A horrified hush fell over the entire monster world.

Brian turned around. His feeling of excitement seemed to drop right out of his body. It was replaced by blind terror. Rumbling toward the small, cowering monster was the largest being he'd seen this side of Arnold Schwarzenegger. His pecs were like granite boulders, his thighs like sculpted gas tanks — even his ears seemed to have biceps. When he opened his mouth, the muscles in his neck worked furiously.

"Arnold," he bellowed, "when Boy wants something he gets it. When Boy requests a favor, you should be honored."

"Snik, please, you got to believe me," the monster sniveled. "I tried, but I got bad knees, real bad knees. Too many stairs!"

Snik flexed his swelling, rippling arms. "Arnold, where would you like your head?"

With an awesome, quick movement, Snik grabbed Arnold's head — and pulled it off his shoulders. Casually Snik began bouncing it on the floor. "Would you like me to play basketball with it?"

Brian's face was frozen in horror. As Arnold's head slapped repeatedly to the floor, it continued to speak. "Aaaah! Snik, I hate when people bounce my head. It hurts!"

"Or would you prefer me to show you some of my ball-handling skills?"

"No . . . NO . . . *NOOOOOO!*" Arnold's head screamed, as Snik gleefully passed it around his neck and spun it on his finger. "Snik! Make it stop!"

With a self-satisfied smile, Snik stopped the spinning and put Arnold's head back in his hands.

"Thank you, thank you," the head said. "You're a good man and one heck of a ball handler." Arnold placed his head back on his shoulders, stumbling around dizzily.

"Remember what I said," Snik warned. "When

Boy wants something he gets it. Never forget that."

Brian felt his own legs wobbling as he chased after Maurice, who was now running down a corridor. Brian was full of questions — but more than anything else, he wanted to know who this "Boy" was. He'd have to remember to ask later.

They raced across catwalks, slid down chutes, and climbed ladders. Maurice finally stopped at the bottom of a long staircase.

"Here we are," he announced.

"Atlanta already?" Brian asked.

"Relax, you'll get your mileage, you'll get your upgrade."

He scampered up the stairs, disappearing into the darkness above. Brian climbed after him, taking the steps two at a time, heading for the pitch-black entrance to someone's bedroom —

BONK! He bounced back as his head hit against an unseen ceiling.

Instantly Maurice reached down, grabbed Brian's collar, and yanked him through.

Brian's head protruded through a carpeted floor. He brushed a dirty sock off his forehead. Maurice's head was beside him, looking around at a quiet bedroom from their vantage point beneath the bed.

"This is someone else's house!" Brian said.

Maurice rolled his eyes. "Duhhhh, where'd ya park the squad car, Dick Tracy?"

As an ankle flopped down off the bed and hung in front of them, Brian smiled wickedly. He reached out to grab it.

But Maurice seized his wrist. "Wait! Good instinct, but too primitive."

He lifted the front of the bed and they both climbed out. Brian felt strange being in someone else's room — especially one as perfectly clean as this one. He stood by the bed with Maurice. Together they gazed down at a blissful, fresh-scrubbed, sleeping boy.

"Isn't he a sweet kid?" Maurice whispered. "I bet he's dreaming about puppies and his favorite baseball player."

"Yeah," Brian whispered back.

"Well, not for long." Maurice reared his head back, took a deep breath — and let out a wail that almost blew the roof off.

"WEEEEEEEEEAAAAAAAAAAHHHHHH!" Brian covered his ears. The sleeping boy's eyes snapped open. The color drained from his face. And when he let out his own ear-splitting shriek, Brian could swear his hair was standing on end.

Brian soon found out that the fun had just begun. They climbed in and out of the monster world, from bedroom to bedroom. Maurice finger-painted on walls. Brian tossed clothes around. Maurice tracked mud on a white carpet. Brian took out records and put them in the wrong jackets, while Maurice scratched others with the tone arm. Brian pulled a club out of a golf bag marked *Dad's* and bent it. Maurice put a skateboard on the top of a stairway and covered it with a shirt. They both exploded a tomato in a microwave, smeared chocolate and grease all over a kitchen, turned on taps, squirted toothpaste, flooded bathrooms. They hid house keys, car keys, combs, brushes, batteries. . . .

With each visit Brian got bolder, trying to outdo Maurice. Finally, in a bathroom in Boston, Brian was hit with his finest inspiration. As Maurice watched admiringly, he took a container of baby powder and emptied it into the fan section of a blow dryer.

Maurice threw his arms around him. "Brilliant!" he screamed.

When they escaped back into the underworld, they collapsed in a fit of laughter. "That's what it's all about down here!" Maurice said. "Every night's the big one, the Super Bowl, the World Series. We exist to sow the seeds of family discontent. *We're* the reason kids get locked in their rooms, we're the reason brothers hate their sisters, and we're the reason parents send their kids to camp." He did a little dance of joy. "Oh, I love it! I'm alive!"

Suddenly Brian stopped laughing. An idea blasted into his head, a truly divine inspiration. "Maurice?" he said, welling up with excitement. "Is there any way we can make a special visit?"

Maurice trembled with delight. "You're too good, just too good to be true! Where have you been sleeping all my life?"

Brian sped off in the direction of Massachusetts. They were going to pop in on one of Brian's closest acquaintances.

Ronnie Coleman.

Chapter 10

A war zone.

That was the only way to describe the room. Socks were draped over pants, which were draped over chairs, which had fallen on their sides on top of baseball equipment, which lay on top of more clothes. There was no place to walk, and only one sign of life — Ronnie Coleman, fast asleep under a mass of covers.

Brian's shoulders drooped. "There's nothing to do here. Somebody must have beat us to it."

"No," Maurice said sadly. "This is an inside job."

They left the bedroom and scurried quietly downstairs to the Colemans' dark kitchen. A sinkful of filthy dishes greeted them, and flies hovered over the crusty half-finished food on the counter. Licking at some leftover form of meat, a cat lazily swiped its paw at a family of hungry cockroaches.

"Look at this!" Maurice said. "This is *disgusting*!"

Brian pulled open the refrigerator door. The light from within cascaded into the kitchen.

Instantly Maurice turned into a pile of clothes.

Brian couldn't help but giggle. He slammed the door shut.

Maurice popped back up, scowling. He reached behind the refrigerator and grabbed the cord. "Always pull the plug out before you open a fridge!" He yanked the plug himself.

When Brian opened the door again, they both peered inside. Reflected in the dim moonlight, a triple-decker tunafish sandwich sat on the top shelf. It was wrapped in plastic, with Ronnie's name written on it. Next to it was a jar of apple juice.

"That's got to be his lunch," Maurice guessed.

"What can we do to it?" Brian asked.

Beside them, the cat meowed. The sound made Brian's face light up.

He looked at Maurice, who stared back blankly. Brian felt triumphant — now *he* was one step ahead! His eyes drifted toward a can of cat food in the open cupboard.

Maurice's befuddled look turned into a huge grin. As Brian grabbed one can and looked for a can opener, Maurice opened another with his teeth.

In minutes they had removed the tunafish from the sandwich. Scoop by scoop, they replaced it with the sticky brown glop from the cat food cans.

Wrapping the plastic around the sandwich, they slid it back on the refrigerator shelf.

They zipped back upstairs, trying hard not to explode with laughter. And when they finally dove into the underworld, they fell to the ground, howling.

"Oh! I wish I could be there when he tastes it!" Maurice cried.

"I feel like I've been on vacation for a week!" Brian exclaimed.

Just how long *had* he been down there, he wondered. He glanced quickly at his watch — and immediately sat bolt upright. "Oh, no! My dad gets up in ten minutes!"

Maurice took a look for himself. "Man! The sun rises in five." He reached into his jacket pocket and handed Brian a pair of sunglasses. "I can't bear to see anyone go up there without protection. Those U.V.'s can do a lot of damage — if you know what I mean."

"Thanks," Brian said, putting on the glasses.

"Visiting hours are over at dawn, and unless you're looking for a new residence and a pair of horns, we'd better book."

They ran to the stairs below the Stevenson house. As Maurice quickly whisked Brian up toward the attic bedroom, neither of them could see what was happening in Cleveland, Atlanta, and Boston. A mortified, tearful girl cowering in a wrecked kitchen as her parents read her the riot act. A father slipping down a staircase on a skateboard. A six-year-old girl holding a blow dryer, her face caked with a layer of powder.

It was all in a night's work, the greatest night of Brian's life. And when he finally popped up into his room just before sunrise, there was only one thought on his mind.

Going back for more.

Snap, snap, snap.

Brian opened his eyes. Through his sunglasses he saw a geometry triangle hitting the desk by his face. Attached to it was Mr. Finn's arm.

"Good morning, Mr. Stevenson," the teacher said. "Having a nice nap?"

Brian frantically adjusted his body, lifting his head off the desk. He hadn't slept after getting back that morning, and he could barely remember getting himself to school.

"No, no, don't let us interrupt your little siesta," Mr. Finn went on. "We wouldn't want to disturb you or bore you with the single most significant geometric equation that separates modern man from Neanderthal man. The one theorem that — "

The ringing of the bell broke off Mr. Finn's sentence. He held out his arm as Brian got up to leave. "I'll see you back here at three-thirty," he said.

"Sure," Brian replied dejectedly.

Mr. Finn put his arm down. His face showed a hint of concern. "And get some rest."

* * *

There was only one period that Brian had no trouble being awake in — lunch. He felt his blood pounding as he saw Ronnie sit at a table, innocently toting his lunch bag. Brian quietly sat two tables away and waited.

"Hey, what's with the glasses, Rip Van Winkle?" came an amused voice.

Kiersten! What timing. The last thing Brian needed was a distraction. He shrugged and said, "I had a late night."

"Oh, really? Up late working on *your* project?"

Brian watched Ronnie carefully upwrap his sandwich and set it down. He twisted the cap off his apple juice.

"Actually I never looked at it that way," Brian muttered.

"Well, *mine*'s finished," Kiersten said proudly.

"Great."

Brian wasn't hearing a word of the conversation. Ronnie had both hands around the sandwich now. He lifted it to his mouth. Taking a deep breath, he opened wide.

And with one huge, hungry chomp, he dug his teeth into the heart of the heaping brown mass.

One chew, two . . . three. . . . Ronnie's eyes sprang open. His face blanched. He took one more chew, just to make sure. . . .

"YEEEEUUUUCCHHHH!" Jumping from his seat, he spat the sandwich out.

Fortunately for his friends, he had missed them completely.

But unfortunately for Ronnie, he had scored a bull's-eye with someone else.

Mr. Dutton.

Brian felt a grin stretch across his face. And as the soiled principal led Ronnie away by the shoulder, Brian noticed that Kiersten was smiling, too.

Chapter 11

Brian paced his room. Outside, thunder cracked and rain pelted his window, but he barely noticed.

Where was Maurice? he wondered. Did I do something to keep him away?

Brian went around the room, adjusting the colored gels he had put over the lights to cut down their intensity. There was no chance they would have any effect on Maurice.

So why wasn't he there yet?

He knelt down by the bed and tried to peer into the shadow.

Nothing. Total blackness.

Out of curiosity, he reached his hand under the bed. He held it just above the floor. Then he gently dropped it downward.

And downward. . . .

It had gone through — without any help! He whipped it back and stared at it with a mixture of happiness and fear. Only monsters were supposed to be able to do that.

He glanced back at the shadow, then passed his hand through it again — slowly, past the wrist, up to the elbow. . . .

Thunk. Suddenly he lurched forward, his head bouncing against the mattress.

He hurtled downward into the darkness, coming to a stop halfway down the underworld staircase. Maurice had hold of his arm.

"A natural!" Maurice exclaimed. "A no-holds-barred, dyed-in-the-wool, no-assembly-required natural! I knew you had it in you!"

"What do you mean?" Brian asked.

"What do you think? I thought *I* caught on quick, but you! You're already moving through shadows!"

Brian had a creepy feeling. "No, I'm not. You pulled me through."

"Believe what you want to believe, Bri, but it was a lot easier pulling you through tonight than it was last night." He yanked Brian down the stairs. "Come on, Bri, baby. I have to show you something."

They went down the stairway, across a gangplank, and through an old, carved oak arch. Inside the arch, high wooden shelves stretched out in all directions, each carefully labeled: THUMBTACKS, STICKPINS, SUPERGLUE, SINGLE SOCKS, CLAY, MUD, GREASE, NAIR, SKATEBOARDS.

"Bri, I'm telling you," Maurice said, "there's enough trouble on these shelves to send America's youth to their rooms for life. My heart pounds when I wander through here."

He led Brian down a long aisle, passing shelves labeled PENS, SUNGLASSES, SINGLE EARRINGS. In the midst of one shelf, Maurice stopped to take something out of a giant box marked TICKETS. "Look at this! Some poor disco bunny shelled out fifty bucks to see a Bruce Springsteen concert and she *lost* her ticket!"

Brian's brow furrowed. "Is all this stuff stolen?"

SHHHPPPLLAAAAT! Brian and Maurice jumped back as a heavy, orange plastic bag fell in front of them. "What do you think we are? Bandits, pirates?" a voice cackled overhead.

They looked up to the top of a long pole. A gap-toothed old monster smiled down at them, straddling the pole on a platform like a crow's nest. His feet rested on pedals, which moved his pole back and forth. He shrugged helplessly and giggled. "It's all *lost!*"

As he burst into laughter, Brian picked up the plastic bag. He realized it wasn't orange at all — it was clear. The orange color was from goldfish. Dead goldfish, hundreds of them all neatly packed in rows.

"So what do you do with these?" Brian asked, his lip curled in disgust.

"Replace the live ones with dead ones," Maurice answered. "Pretty ingenious, huh? Pet responsibility lectures — my favorite!"

The grizzled old monster pedaled away, humming. Brian dropped the bag, his eyes focusing on something much more interesting — a box marked

GIRLIE MAGAZINES. "Wow! You get to look at those?"

He pulled one out. "I found a Playboy once when I was trash digging. Boy, my mom — "

Suddenly another idea hit Brian. A perfect place to put the magazine. He rolled it up and stuck it in his back pocket. "There's a stop I want to make," he said.

Brian tiptoed across Todd's bedroom. Silently he opened the top drawer of his dresser. He pushed aside some clothes, inserted the magazine, then closed the drawer. On his way back to the shadow, he looked down at Todd, sleeping soundly.

"Explain *that* to your mom," he whispered, then hopped back into the underworld.

Maurice was quieter than usual as they climbed down the stairs and walked along a hallway. "Listen, Brian," he finally said. "No offense, but I'm getting a little tired of visiting all these guys. Aren't there any chicks in your life?"

Brian wasn't expecting that. "Huh?"

"Chicks! Broads! Girls! Don't you know any besides your mother?"

"Do me a favor, will you, Maurice? Try to keep the language a little less vulgar. And I'd appreciate it if you kept my mother out of it!"

"Excuse me, Mr. Shakespeare!" Maurice said with a snort.

"I do know one girl."

Maurice's mouth curled into a grin. "One is better than none!"

Slowly Maurice lifted the bed. Brian looked around, feeling his stomach flutter as if there were a jackhammer inside.

Outside a dog barked. There was a movement on top of the bed, a shifting of position. Brian and Maurice froze.

But the movement stopped, and both of them climbed into the room. "So, what's this Kiersten chick like?" Maurice asked, glancing down at her sleeping form. "Personally I'm a wart-and-mole kind of guy."

Brian wasn't listening. He had never looked at Kiersten's face closely before, never really *seen* it. Part of him felt like running away, as if Kiersten's room was the last place on earth he belonged.

But part of him just wanted to stand there and admire.

"Hey!"

Maurice's shout snapped him back to reality. Brian tore his glance away from Kiersten. "She's neat," he said. "But she's a girl. Real smart. Always knows the answer, always raises her hand — "

"Always has her homework done?"

"Yeah." Brian's attention wandered back to her. But this time, he was distracted by something out of the corner of his eye. Something taped to her mirror.

It was a photo of Brian — the Polaroid he had taken of himself in class!

A warm feeling washed over him, catching him completely by surprise. "I don't believe it," he said softly. "She likes me. I thought she hated me."

"Why would anyone hate you?" Maurice remarked. "All you are is ugly."

"It's just that since we moved here I haven't been able to make friends with anyone other than you. I didn't think anyone cared about me — least of all Kiersten."

"Brian, everyone cares. They just have different ways of showing it." With that, he peeled a mole off his face and handed it to Brian.

Brian gave him a dirty look. His eyes wandered down to the top of her dresser, where a folder stuck out of her open schoolbag. He pulled it out and opened it.

It was her science report. Perfectly typed. He leafed through it, glancing at some of the crisp sentences and the lifelike drawings.

Brains as well as looks. This was too good to be true.

"What's this?" Maurice asked, peering down at a box on the floor.

"A cactus box," Brian answered, still in a daze.

Maurice flipped up the sliding wall of the box — sending a stream of light out the side.

"YEEEEOOOOW!" he shrieked, jumping away. He held his arm out in pain. Smoke drifted upward from his seared flesh — and the horns on his head grew another inch.

"It's sunlight!" Maurice cried.

"Close. It's a sunlamp."

"Same difference."

"You okay?"

"Never felt better. Getting toasted is a hobby of mine."

She likes me. The thought kept flashing through Brian's head. For the first time all day, he wasn't obsessed with the monster world, or Maurice. He turned back to look at Kiersten, planning what he'd say to her in school.

Suddenly he was hit in the face with a T-shirt. He spun around to see Maurice tossing the clothes out of Kiersten's drawers.

Brian ran across the room. "No! Give her a break!"

"I already gave her a break," Maurice retorted. "I didn't repaint her room."

Brian gathered up the clothes, armful by armful. Frantically trying to stuff them back in the drawers, he wasn't able to see that Maurice had moved on to something else.

Kiersten's report.

Maurice held it in his left hand and smiled. Then he lifted his right hand. Slowly the hand dissolved — and became the muzzle of a snarling, dagger-toothed dog! With a ferocious chomp, it tore into the report.

As the thunder rumbled fiercely outside, Brian never heard the sound of crumpling paper.

BOOOOOOM!

Eric shook as he tiptoed down the hallway. He couldn't take the thunder. Not all alone. Not after seeing a real, live monster in his room only four nights ago. Maybe he could just sneak into his mom and dad's bedroom, nuzzle in between them, or curl up on the floor. If he did it quietly enough, they wouldn't even wake up. . . .

"You want to do this and that, here and there. Why don't you get a job?"

Eric stopped in his tracks. It was his dad's voice.

"Glen!" his mom replied. "How can you say that?"

Better try another approach, Eric thought.

He headed for the attic stairs to Brian's room. Brian might make fun of him, but he was used to that. It would be better than being in that creepy room by himself.

Slowly he climbed up. The attic room was pitch-black at the top of the stairs. He poked his head through the floor.

"Brian?"

There was no answer. Thunder bellowed in the distance, and a bolt of lightning lit up a sleeping form on Brian's bed. How can he sleep through that? Eric wondered.

"Brian? Can I have the flashlight?"

He groped awkwardly through the darkness until he bumped into the bed. His hand reached up toward the pillow, trying to locate Brian's shoulder. He felt something under the covers and shook it.

It sure didn't feel like a shoulder. Eric fumbled around some more, but Brian's body felt like a big, shapeless lump.

Panic ripped through him. He pulled the covers back.

Underneath them were Brian's pillows, shaped like a sleeping person. He backed away in horror.

His brother was gone.

Chapter 12

A monster ran by carrying a VCR. Two of them descended a ladder, lugging stereo components. Still another screamed with laughter as it dragged a smashed TV set up another ladder.

Lamps, vases, aquariums, crystal, paintings — if it was expensive and fragile, the monsters had brought it down from someone's room. But Brian ignored the chaos around him as he walked with Maurice.

"You shouldn't have messed up her room," he scolded.

"Brian," Maurice said, "never get emotionally involved with a victim. It's tough killing someone's goldfish when you really care for that person."

"But she liked me! I can't wait to see her tomorrow."

The loud crack of a bat interrupted him, followed by the shattering of glass.

A sudden raucous cheer echoed through the underworld. Brian and Maurice ran toward it.

They passed into a cavernous chamber, where a large monster was taking practice swings with a bat. In front of him was a baseball field — sort of. Targets had been set up in the outfield: porcelain lamps, vases, platters, furniture.

As the monster placed his feet next to a china serving dish, where home plate should have been, an announcer's voice rang out: *"Stepping into the batter's box is a man whose red-hot stick has him in the midst of a two-hundred-eighty-seven-game porcelain-lamp hitting streak. Let's hear it for Tank!"*

The crowd roared as Tank settled in. The pitcher took his signs and wound up. He let fly with a fastball.

WHACK!

The ball streaked through the air. The fans stood on their feet, their eyes following the ball's arc.

CRASSSSSH! A porcelain lamp became history as the ball smashed it to pieces.

The stands exploded with cheering. *"Oh, myyyyy!"* came the announcer's voice. *"The streak lives on!"*

Brian felt himself pulsing with the crowd's excitement. He watched Maurice run over to a bin full of baseball gloves.

"This one'll fit," Maurice said, tossing a glove to Brian.

Brian caught it. "How do you play?"

Maurice pointed to the objects in the outfield. "We get the stuff from people's houses, we smash the stuff, then we put the stuff back. It's called Monsterball — we do the bashing, you get the thrashing!"

With that, he ran onto the outfield. Brian grabbed the mitt and joined him. The inning seemed to last for hours, but Brian didn't mind. He chased after line drives, winding his way through the debris. Lamps shattered, plates smashed, chairs splintered. But both he and Maurice made diving, spectacular catches. They whooped and hollered over the crowd noise, giving each other high-fives after each catch.

Then, with two out, the throng fell silent. Up to the plate stalked a gargantuan creature, lugging a bat the size of an oak tree. His shoulders were like a side of beef, his hands the size of seat cushions. He made José Canseco look like Pee-wee Herman.

"The beast holds the Monsterball record for inflicting more than seven-hundred-thousand-dollars worth of damage with one mighty swing of the bat," the voice continued. *"Ladies and gentlemen, the almighty Pumpkin Head . . . Doctor of Devastation-n-n-n-n!"*

Brian swallowed. Something about this creature reminded him of Ronnie Coleman. He tapped his glove. He was going to catch this ball if it was the last thing he did.

The pitcher let loose a searing fastball. With a swing so strong Brian felt the wind in the outfield, Pumpkin Head missed.

The objects around Brian rattled. He gulped.

Pumpkin Head was furious now. Steam rose from his ears, eyes, nose, and mouth.

On the next pitch Pumpkin Head coiled back. His beady eyes on fire, he whipped the bat around.

CRRRRRRRRRRRRAACKKKKKK!

The ball tore through the sky like a comet. Outfielders chased after it, laughing at their own meager efforts.

But not Brian. He sped after the ball, his feet barely touching the ground. As the ball disappeared into the murky darkness outside the field, the expressions on his teammates' faces turned to horror. They began clearing the field, running away. They murmured to each other and pointed to Brian.

Even if Brian had seen them, he wouldn't have cared. He wasn't going to let the ball out of his sight.

It fell with a clank at the top of a staircase. Brian scampered upward, spiraling into the darkness. The shadows became deeper, and slowly enveloped the stairs.

Brian stopped, clutching a banister. He pulled out his flashlight and flipped it on. Swinging it all around, he searched for the ball.

And that's when he felt the hand reaching over his shoulder. Not like a human hand, more like a steel vise. It plucked the flashlight away from him. Brian spun around in a panic. The light beam cut crazy patterns in the darkness, revealing nothing.

Suddenly he felt a giant thumb closing over one

ear, a forefinger closing over the other. Like a piece of trash about to be discarded, he felt himself rising off the stairs, over the railing. . . .

He flailed with his arms and legs, but it made no difference. Below him, a bottomless pit of blackness waited, open-mouthed.

And in front of him, attached to the arm that was about to release him to his death, was a monster he had hoped he'd never see again.

Snik.

Chapter 13

Snik clamped his teeth on the flashlight and un-screwed it. The beam went out.

A scream welled up inside Brian. He opened his mouth, but the scream was locked inside.

Another voice suddenly cut through the dark-ness. "He's with me, Snik!"

Maurice! Brian felt a tiny glimmer of hope.

Snik ignored the plea. With his free hand, he crushed the flashlight batteries. Acid spurted out onto his arm. He licked it off and dropped the bat-teries over the railing. They disappeared into the darkness below Brian.

Brian didn't hear them hit bottom. He went rigid with fear. His head rang with pain. His eyes clung desperately to Maurice.

"He's the new kid," Maurice explained to Snik.

"Maurice," Snik grumbled, "he shouldn't come this close to the stairway. I could break his puny neck."

Maurice hopped onto the banister and whispered into Snik's ear, "Headless people have limited *potential*, Snik. He's with me, and Boy isn't going to want him hurt."

Snik lifted Brian back over the railing, but kept him suspended in the air. "Too much for you, Maurice?" he asked. "You need help, I think."

"No, Snik," Maurice answered firmly. "I'll take care of him."

"You'd better."

Just then, high above them, a set of doors split open. A silhouette appeared, lit from behind. Snik and Maurice looked up.

Brian felt himself tumble to the ground as Snik let go of his head. Immediately Maurice pulled Brian to his feet and practically pushed him down the stairs. Brian stumbled to the bottom, where Maurice shoved him through an archway and out of Snik's sight.

Brian leaned against a wall and caught his breath. "Who *was* that guy, Maurice?"

"Who, Snik?" Maurice said. "Big talker — all mouth. He gets up on the wrong side of the bed three hundred sixty-five days a year." He gave Brian a meaningful look. "You learn to stay away from him and his staircase."

"No kidding."

At the top of the stairway, far above Brian and Maurice's line of sight, the ominous shape drew back into the shadows. The mighty doors boomed shut.

* * *

Todd looked at Eric anxiously as they walked down a school hallway the next morning. "You sure he wasn't there?" he asked.

"Sure I'm sure!" Eric replied. "The room was empty!"

"Was the window open?"

"I don't know. I didn't check."

"Hmm . . . maybe he went outside. Maybe he stepped outside for some air. I'll bet that's it."

"At four in the morning?"

"I know! We should spy on him — run a surveillance!"

Eric stiffened. "There he is."

At the other end of the hallway, Brian didn't notice his brother. He *did* notice that his pants were a little looser on him than the last time he wore them. Which was strange, considering his mom had been thinking of putting them away for Eric.

Oh well, he thought, looks like I'll just have to eat more at the monster dining hall next time. He walked past a row of lockers, weaving a little from lack of sleep. But when he saw Kiersten pulling books out of her locker, a smug grin crossed his ashen, exhausted face. His walk became a confident strut.

"Hey, Kiersten," he said nonchalantly. "Dream about anyone special last night?"

He leaned back, ready for her to drape her arms around him.

But Kiersten just snickered. "I'd dream about Thomas Edison before I'd dream about you." She gave him a quick head-to-toe look. "And why are you wearing Ronnie Coleman's pants?"

Stunned, Brian stood there as she walked away. He looked down at his pants. They weren't Ronnie's, but they might as well have been — they bunched up at the waist, and the legs hung over his shoes. He wondered if his mom had let them out.

The bell rang, and Brian ran toward science class. When he got there, he saw Mr. Finn, Kiersten, Ronnie, and a group of other students huddled around a lab table. In front of them was a box containing Kiersten's night-blooming cactus. Kiersten's schoolbag lay next to it.

Mr. Finn inspected the experiment, then looked up at Kiersten. "Do you have your research paper?"

"Yes I do, Mr. Finn," Kiersten replied with a proud grin. She reached into her schoolbag. Suddenly her eyes glazed over as her hand clasped around it.

With a shocked, disbelieving look, she pulled out the crumpled, chewed-up pile of sheets.

Brian's mouth hung open. *Maurice* must have done that!

"I — I guess my dog chewed it up," Kiersten stammered.

"Oh, right," Ronnie replied with a snicker. "You don't even have a dog."

Some of the other students laughed, but Mr. Finn's face was somber with disappointment. He frowned at Kiersten. "You know I have to give you a zero if there's no report. I have no choice, Kiersten."

"It wasn't my fault," Kiersten pleaded.

Mr. Finn looked as if he'd heard that one a thousand times. "I'm sorry," he said.

Kiersten's pain seemed to shoot right through Brian, as if they were connected by an electric current. His head hung down. Slowly he turned away. He could never forgive himself. Kiersten had failed the subject she loved best, and it was all because of him.

Chapter 14

Eric climbed up the trellis outside his house — carefully, since he was still in his school clothes. Below him, Todd looked up impatiently. "What's he doing?" he called, trying to keep his voice just above a whisper.

Eric pulled himself up the final few feet and peered through the attic window. "Sleeping," he answered.

"Sleeping? Like asleep? With his eyes closed?"

Eric nodded, his forehead creased with concern. "It's four o'clock in the afternoon. He shouldn't be sleeping."

Todd gave his friend a grave look. "We gotta check this out."

RINNG!

It was dinnertime. Brian hopped out of bed and smothered the alarm clock. He didn't want anyone to know he'd been sleeping since he got back from school.

He ran halfway down the stairs and flinched with pain. The light! It was hurting his eyes. He ran back to get his sunglasses, then headed back down to the dining room.

When he got to the table, Eric was already serving his famous macaroni casserole — made with relish and potato chips mashed in. His mom looked at the casserole dish with a faintly queasy smile.

As Brian slid into his seat, his mom gave him a quizzical look. "Brian, must you wear those sunglasses day and night? I feel like I'm eating dinner with one of Michael Jackson's bodyguards."

"Sorry, Mom," Brian said. He took his glasses off.

No way. This wasn't going to work. It felt as if someone had thrown sand in his eyes. If only it were just a little darker. . . .

Quickly he slipped the glasses back on, got up, and went to the kitchen.

"Brian, are you all right?" Mrs. Stevenson called out.

"Fine, Mom."

The dining room became quiet for a moment as everyone started on their dinner. "Eric," Mrs. Stevenson said, "this is the best macaroni I've ever had! You're going to make someone a good buddy."

Brian found what he needed in the cupboard — two candlesticks, next to a box of matches. He lit the candles and dimmed the lights. Cautiously he removed his sunglasses.

It was going to work. His eyes felt fine.

He brought the candles into the dining room, and set them on the table, and flipped off the overhead light. "There you go. I just figured this place could use a little atmosphere."

As he sat down, his mom beamed with emotion. She reached out and grabbed each son's hand. "I never realized I had such romantic sons."

That night Brian slept with a night-light on. Even if it meant keeping his sunglasses on all night, he was going to make sure Maurice stayed away.

His deep slumber was broken by a crash of broken glass. He snapped awake. The night-light had been shattered.

Standing at the foot of the bed was Maurice. His left hand was now a slingshot.

"Hey, pard," he said. "What's with the light? Something personal?"

"Yeah — you!" Brian shot back.

Maurice looked hurt. "Me? Your only friend in the world?"

"My used-to-be only friend in the world. You chewed up Kiersten's homework! You destroyed it. She got a zero because of you."

"Brian, I was hungry. It just happened that at that exact moment I had a craving for a six-page paper on 'The Daytime Blooming of a Nighttime Cactus.' You can't imagine the heartburn I got from that paper."

"I can't believe you did that. I asked you not to, and you still went ahead and did it anyway!"

"You like her, don't you?"

Brian turned his head away. "No, I don't."

"You do."

"I don't."

"Would it help the boo-boo if I said I was sorry?"

Brian fired an angry glance at him. "Just go back to your dumb underworld and leave me and Eric alone!"

Maurice's eyes drooped. With slumped shoulders, he walked over to the bed. He gave Brian one last pleading look — a look that begged forgiveness.

Brian twisted away defiantly. He felt Maurice begin to pick up the edge of the bed.

What am I doing? Brian suddenly thought. After all the fun we've had, after Maurice had risked himself to save my life, how could I reject him for one mistake?

He turned back to Maurice — just as the overhead light popped on.

The bed dropped. Maurice disintegrated into a pile of clothes.

"Dad!" Brian cried out, louder than he meant to. "What is it?"

Mr. Stevenson walked into the room. His face was blank and tired-looking. "Come downstairs. Your mom and I want to talk to you and Eric."

Something was not right. The face was a big tip-off. So was the tone of voice.

And when Mr. Stevenson put his arm around Brian, he *knew* there was bad news ahead.

Brian's hand reached out for the light switch on the way out, but at the last minute he pulled back.

He wanted the light on while he was gone.

It wasn't until they got to Eric's room that Brian realized his dad was wearing a suit. It hadn't seemed all that strange until he saw his mom sitting on Eric's bed — in a bathrobe.

Brian's and Eric's eyes were glued to Mr. Stevenson as he paced the room. "We wanted to talk to you two because your mother and I have come to a decision, and it affects all of us."

"We feel you're both grown-up enough to understand," Mrs. Stevenson added, looking at her sons sadly.

Brian felt his insides begin to crumble. He saw his brother's eyes fill with worry.

His dad stood still and heaved a big sigh. "Mom and I have decided to live separately for a while."

The words landed on Brian like a concrete block. He had known for a long time that things weren't great between his parents, but he didn't expect *this*.

"A business trip?" Eric piped up in an uncertain voice.

Brian glared at him. "No! Can't you see? They're getting a divorce!" He was shocked by the bitterness in his own voice.

Eric cast a frightened look at his mother.

"No, we're *not* getting a divorce," she said firmly. "It's just that, for your father and I to work things out, we have to be apart for a while."

"It's like a trial separation," Mr. Stevenson added.

Brian nodded. "It's what you do *before* you get a divorce."

"So Dad's not leaving," Eric said with a nervous giggle. "Good."

Mr. Stevenson leaned down to his younger son. "Eric, listen to me. I'm going to have to live in the city for a while. We hope it won't be for long."

"You don't have to go," Eric said.

"Yes, Eric. I do." Mr. Stevenson gave a half smile. "Look, we'll talk every day. Believe me, things always work out for the best."

"I'll be good!" Eric pleaded. "I promise I'll be better — you won't have to go live in the city. I promise. I'll be better. Brian, too — he'll stop being bad, he promises! Right?" He turned a desperate face to Brian.

Brian looked away, ignoring him.

"Eric," Mrs. Stevenson said gently, "it's not your fault, or Brian's fault — or *anybody's* fault. It's nobody's fault."

Silence hung in the air. Brian could feel all eyes on him. He stared into the floor, letting the hurt and anger tumble around inside him.

"Brian," his dad said very softly, "are you all right?"

"Sure, Dad," Brian replied, his throat barely letting the words out. "I'll be fine."

What he didn't want to say was that being alive just didn't seem worth it anymore.

Chapter 15

As Brian walked back to his room, he felt stunned. The walls of the house seemed to disappear. He didn't notice the attic stairs as he climbed. But as he walked into his room, the sight of the clothes on the floor jarred him back to reality. Maurice had probably heard the whole thing.

He sighed and lifted his hand to the light switch. This wasn't what he wanted to do a few minutes ago, but it was too painful to be alone right now. He needed *someone* to talk to.

With a flick of his wrist, the light went out.

Maurice instantly popped back to life. Brian shuffled past him and sat on the bed. Maurice sat beside him. He pulled his entire slingshot hand off and gave it to Brian. "Here."

"Nah," Brian said, waving him away.

Maurice shrugged and put his hand back on. Then he said, "I heard it all."

"Pretty lousy, huh?"

"Yeah, not too good."

"I hate them."

Maurice frowned. "No, you don't. At least you have a family. Believe it or not, you're the only real friend I have. Why do you think I keep coming back? If I didn't like you, I'd have your parents blaming you for shooting Abe Lincoln."

Despite his gloomy mood, Brian chuckled.

"Come on down," Maurice said, gesturing toward the floor. "It'll cheer you up."

"I don't feel like being cheery."

"Bri, baby. Games, snacks, pranks — it'll take your mind off the hurt. We could take a look at Kiersten, maybe bring her flowers. Or go see Ronnie Coleman and loosen the bolts on his furniture."

Brian felt his resolve weakening. His lips turned up into a smile.

"Come on, we'll make it quick," Maurice pressed. "It'll be good for your bones. I promise."

Things were starting to become clearer for Brian. There was no doubt about it — his life had reached bottom. His parents were splitting, his brother was a basket case, he had become a hazard to everyone he knew at school, and his only friend had horns and lived in a monster world.

Face the facts, Brian said to himself. No matter what you do, things will never be normal again. So why spend the rest of your life wallowing in gloom?

When he turned to Maurice, his sadness was mixed with a spark of excitement. "Okay," he said. "Let's go."

"All *riiiight!*" Maurice shouted.

Wearing the only two smiles in the entire Stevenson house that night, they jumped into the shadow.

At the bottom of the stairs, they were almost trampled by a stampede of monsters.

"Hey, where's the party?" Maurice yelled.

"Night-light out at the Gubermans'!" a voice answered.

Maurice turned to Brian, his eyes dancing. "Fate, Brian. It's all about fate."

Brian tried to feel the same level of intensity — but somehow, it just wasn't there. Maybe he'd start feeling it at the Gubermans', whoever they were.

Maurice barged through the middle of the throng, going up the stairway to the Guberman house. "Heads up!" he yelled. "New guy! Excuse me, coming through!"

Finally Brian felt his adrenalin start to pump. This was going to be great. There would be a mob of monsters in the house — they'd be able to really turn the place inside out!

As they popped up through the shadow, Brian noticed that this room was somehow different. There was none of the usual mess — no sneakers, no posters or games on the floor. Puzzled, Brian climbed into the room.

Maurice and a half-dozen other monsters were crowded around the bed, blocking Brian's view. Instead of shouting, they were making soft, garbled noises. Probably just trying to decide who shrieks first, Brian thought. Grinning, he pushed Maurice aside and looked over his shoulder.

His eyes widened. It wasn't a bed at all they were looking at. It was a crib. Inside it was a tiny baby, fast asleep.

Brian whirled around. Monsters were trashing the room — tearing diapers, putting sand in the bady powder, removing the battery from the smoke detector.

This can't be happening, Brian said to himself. Not *here*!

Just then Maurice called out to him. "Give it a shot." He pointed to the baby. "Scare him!"

"Maurice, come on," Brian said, fidgeting. "It's a little baby."

"Hey, it's our duty to break them in while they're young!"

Timidly Brian leaned forward. The monsters leaned forward with him, watching and waiting.

"Boo," Brian said softly. He wiggled his fingers at the sleeping child. "Boo."

Together the monsters let out a groan of disgust. "What are you, the tooth fairy?" Maurice asked.

One of the group took a deep breath and let out a banshee wail: "YEEEEEEEEAAHHHHHH!"

The baby didn't budge. Horrified, Brian pulled the monster away from the crib. "Stop it! Leave him alone."

Maurice gave the others a nervous glance. They murmured amongst themselves. Brian heard one of them call him a wimp.

Another monster leaned over the crib. Suddenly his eyes and mouth bulged out from his face and his skin drew back. The face was so ugly even Brian could barely look. He reached out and pulled the monster back. This was getting out of control. "Come on. Stop it!"

"Brian, relax," Maurice said. "Fear is an important character builder. We can't have this new generation growing up not believing in monsters."

"But, Maurice, this is cruel," Brian pleaded.

Just then a sleepy cry began to pierce the air. The baby had started to move. Brian felt rage welling up inside him. Fun was fun, but this wasn't fair.

He ran to the wall and flicked on a light switch. Nothing happened. Someone must have shorted it, he realized. Still, there was *some* light coming into the room.

Under the door. That's where it was. Brian raced to the door handle.

"Brian!" Maurice shouted in dismay.

But Brian wasn't taking any prisoners. He swung the door open.

Light from the hall cascaded into the room. Silently the monsters all became clothes — *lots* of clothes. Brian smiled in triumph.

Until he looked down.

Where his arm had just been, there was nothing but a dangling shirtsleeve.

As fast as his legs could carry him, Brian ran out of the house and into the cold autumn night.

Chapter 16

Maurice stepped backward as the hulking shadow engulfed him. He knew he'd be punished for returning to the underworld without Brian.

"You did bad, Maurice," Snik growled. "We almost had him and *you* lost him. He knows our secrets!"

Snik grabbed a bottle of mustard off a nearby table. With an angry snarl, he crushed it in his hand.

"Who would believe him?" Maurice asked. "Leave him alone. He's harmless."

"But Boy needs a playmate. He's very lonely."

Snik slowly approached Maurice. With each step, he grabbed ketchup bottles, cola bottles, salt and pepper shakers, napkin holders — crushing them one by one.

"I'll take care of it," Maurice said. "Give me one more chance."

"It's too late, Maurice. You've failed!"

Maurice felt his knees buckle as Snik's enormous, food-stained hand reached for his face.

Brian sneaked around the back of the Stevensons' house. Not one light was on, which filled him with relief — for more than one reason. He'd be able to sneak inside unnoticed, *and* he'd have two intact hands while doing it.

He made his way to the trellis and started climbing — until he heard a rustling noise in the trees. He backed away, then saw something fall to the ground with a thud.

Something large and dark. With a voice exactly like Todd's.

"Ouch!" Todd cried out. He struggled out of his sleeping bag.

"Todd," Brian whispered, walking over to him. "Your parents lock you out?"

"Bri!" Todd said. He pulled a flashlight out of his sleeping bag. Brian tried to duck away, but the beam hit him right on the arm.

As the arm disappeared from Brian's sleeve, Todd's eyes popped open in terror. Half in his sleeping bag, he tried to stand up and back away.

Before Brian could say anything, Todd was out of his bag and sprinting down the street. In the darkness, Brian's arm recovered.

Now Brian was in a blind panic. He scaled the trellis and sneaked into the attic room window. He stumbled down the staircase and went straight to the bathroom. Grabbing the thermometer, he took his temperature. Ninety-eight point six. Good sign — at least *something* about him was normal.

What about his clothes? Why weren't they fitting? He measured himself on a height scale by the door — fifty-two inches. He stood on a weight scale — sixty-four pounds.

Running up to the attic again, he pulled a musty old book off the shelf. He sat on the bed and riffled through the pages. In the near-darkness, he could barely make out the heading *MY HEIGHT AND WEIGHT — BRIAN* on top of one of the pages. He put his eyes up close to the page and followed down, using his index finger: first birthday, second. . . .

He stopped when he came to his eleventh birthday. He moved his finger over to the measurements.

Fifty-four inches tall . . . seventy pounds.

Brian shut the book. The shock cut through him like a knife blade. There was no doubt about it now. It was in black and white.

He was shrinking!

Chapter 17

In the school cafeteria the next day, Eric couldn't eat. All day he'd been in a terrible mood, except for about two seconds — right when he woke up that morning. But by the time his feet had hit the floor, memories of the previous night had flooded back. He couldn't even *look* at his dad at the breakfast table. And for the rest of the day he barely knew where he was, what he was doing.

It wasn't my fault, Mom said so, he kept telling himself. Still, he couldn't believe it. He'd been so *bad* lately — waking them up in the middle of the night, not cleaning up, fighting with Brian. . . .

He fiddled with his food while Todd stuffed his face right next to him.

"I swear, Eric," Todd was saying. "His arm turned into a shirtsleeve when my flashlight hit it. I practically keeled over."

"It was late," Eric replied with a shrug. "You were probably seeing things."

"*Seeing things?* Eric, I have twenty-twenty vision." Excitement seemed to make Todd hungrier. He scooped down the remains of his chocolate pudding. "It's a body-snatcher. That's what it is. Using Brian to prepare the way for the invasion force. Eric, our lives are at stake. You have to believe me!"

But Eric wasn't listening.

Todd turned to face him. "Where is he? Let's go find him. I bet he's hiding inside a cupboard — or maybe even a coffin!"

"Forget it," Eric said dully. "He's home sick."

Todd looked disappointed. He looked back at his empty tray, sighed, and got up to go to the lunch line for seconds.

Thump!

As the last corner of his parents' bed fell to the floor, Brian felt relieved. He sat back and uncurled his fingers from the saw handle.

It was the last wooden leg on the last bed in the house. After all these hours of sawing, every bed was flat against the ground. There were no more shadows.

Maurice was history.

Brian was lucky, and he knew it. His mom hadn't lifted a finger to stop him. All day long, she'd been giving him pitying looks, asking him if he was all right. And when he began sawing off the bed legs in the dark, she smiled sadly and said she understood. Everyone needed a way to deal with pain, she said. And no grief was greater than seeing your parents separate.

Well, it was fine if she believed that. At least she was right about the pain part. And what she didn't know about the monster world wasn't going to hurt her.

Brian picked himself up off the floor. He left a light on in the room, just in case. On the way to the attic steps, he tiptoed into Eric's room. As his brother turned fitfully in his sleep, Brian quietly placed a flashlight on his night-table. No use taking any chances, especially with Eric's state of mind these days.

Before Brian climbed the attic stairs, he flipped on the overhead light in the hallway.

He was exhausted by the time he got to his room. But as he sank onto his mattress, he fought to keep himself awake. He knew his mom would be coming up to her room soon. And he had a feeling she'd make sure to turn off every light in the house.

It would be up to him to wait until she dozed off, then turn them all on again.

Brian was right. She did come upstairs soon. And she did turn the lights out.

But as the house fell completely dark, it was Brian who was fast asleep.

As the grandfather clock in the living room struck two A.M., the Stevenson house was silent. Upstairs, each bed lay tight against the floor. Upstairs, despite the darkness, there was no point of entrance for any monster. Brian's plan was working perfectly.

Upstairs.

Of course, there was no bed downstairs. But there was something happening. A slight movement in the sofa cushions. It might have been a mouse, or a settling of the down feathers.

But none of those things could have caused the cushions to fly into the air. And none of those things could have caused the sofa bed to suddenly spring open.

The legs crashed to the living room floor. Below them was a deep, black, rectangular shadow.

Chapter 18

No, no, leave me alone! Brian thought. Get your hands off me! I don't *want* to go down there anymore, Maurice! I'm through!

Brian passed out of his dream, and into a half-waking state. Now he could tell he was dreaming — yet he knew there really *was* a hand on his shoulder. Someone was trying to wake him up.

"Maurice!" he gasped. He shot up from his bed. "How — ?"

"Eric's gone," his mom's voice answered. "Have you seen him? Do you know where he went?"

He focused his eyes on Mrs. Stevenson's anxious face.

"Gone?" he repeated. "He's gone?"

"If you know anything at all, say it right now."

Brian's mind raced. Eric wouldn't just run away in the middle of the night, no matter how depressed he was. Eric hardly went anywhere unless someone took him. . . .

Someone took him. The words echoed in his

brain. But it couldn't be — there were no beds above the floor, no shadows. No possible way of getting down to the underworld.

Or was there?

"I called Dad," Mrs. Stevenson continued. "You don't think Eric would try to go there, do you?"

Brian shook his head slowly.

She stood up. "Todd's house! Maybe he's there." She ran to the stairs. "Do you know the number?"

Brian shook his head again, trying to control his urge to bolt.

The moment he heard his mom pick up the phone, he flew down the attic stairs and into Eric's room. The sheets had been thrown against the wall. On the floor, the flashlight lay crushed. No *way* Eric did that.

But the bed was exactly as he'd left it. Flat on the floor. Somebody had been in here — somebody who didn't like flashlights. And whoever it was didn't come from under the bed.

At least not *this* bed.

But which? Brian went over the evening in his head. He had gotten *every* bed. Mom's, Eric's, his own. And there were no spare beds. Anyone who ever slept over had to use the —

That was it! Brian raced downstairs into the living room.

When he saw the sofa bed unfolded, he practically fell to his knees in frustration. "No!" he cried.

There was no time to waste. This must be the monsters' way of getting back at him — they figured they couldn't have him so they'd take his little brother.

He ran to the bed. But as he lifted his foot to step in, he stopped.

What was he going to do down there? It was a different ball game now. He couldn't count on Maurice anymore — and even if he could, it wouldn't be enough. The monsters would smash him to pieces.

He was going to need help — and weapons.

He ran back up to his room and stuffed his backpack with the lights he had taken from the garage. Then, racing out the back door, he sprinted the four blocks to Todd's house. He sneaked around back to Todd's first-floor bedroom window and tapped on it — once . . . twice. . . .

Suddenly Todd's head popped up. His sleepy eyes became white with fear when he saw Brian. He held out his fingers in a cross sign.

"Go away!" Todd warned. "You're one of them!"

"Toad, open up," Brian commanded. "I need you and every spare flashlight you can find. They have Eric."

Todd lowered his fingers. "Who has Eric?"

"Monsters kidnapped him."

"Kidnapped him? Which monsters?" Todd opened the window a crack.

His stupid questions! Brian thought. "The — the *little* monsters!"

"You're *nuts!*" Todd cried out. He slammed the window shut and ducked out of sight.

"Toad!" Brian called into the room. "Did you find

a certain not-so-nice *magazine* in your drawer?"

Silence was his answer. Then the window opened slowly and Todd peered out. "No," he said. He shot Brian a dirty look. "My *mother* did! Anyway, how do you know about that?"

"I put it there."

Brian could see the wheels turning in Todd's head. He mulled it over a moment, then cast a quick glance to his bed. When he looked back up at Brian, his face was pale.

"Oh, man," was all he could mutter.

The next stop was Kiersten's house. While Brian tossed pebbles at her room on the second floor, Todd nervously adjusted his backpack. The flashlights inside the pack clanked noisily.

Right away Kiersten appeared at the window. She looked down at them, confused.

"Hi, Kiersten," Brian said cheerfully.

"Brian! What's wrong?" she replied.

"You're not going to believe this, but I need your key to get into the supply room. It's an emergency. I need some lights."

Kiersten looked at him as if he'd lost his mind. "Now? What is the matter with you, Brian Stevenson? Do you have any idea what time it is?"

Brian held his breath. He knew he had to be direct. "Kiersten," he said firmly. "I've seen the picture."

"What picture?"

"The one on the mirror over your dresser."

Kiersten's shocked eyes darted into the room and back.

"Come on, Kiersten, let me in," Brian pleaded. "I can explain."

"All right," she said with a sigh, "but this better be worth it."

She let them in, and Brian explained everything. But the more she heard, the less she believed. Finally she shook her head and said, "You expect me to believe that? It defies every rule known to the scientific mind — and mine!"

Brian crouched beside the bed. "Here, watch this."

He put his hand into the shadow. His arm disappeared up to the elbow. "Go ahead. Try it, Miss DEE-vo."

Kiersten tentatively reached toward the shadow and stubbed her hand.

When she pulled it back, Brian looked for a reaction.

There was none. Both she and Todd were speechless.

In minutes, Kiersten packed a backpack with a flashlight and a camping light from her parents' supply closet. When she got back up to her room, Brian waved her over to the bed.

The three of them knelt by the shadow. They adjusted their backpacks.

"Wait a minute," Kiersten suddenly said. "How are we supposed to get into the school? There are no beds there!"

"Kiersten," Brian answered, "will you just trust me for once?"

With one hand, he lifted up the bed. With the other, he held Kiersten's hand. She clutched onto Todd.

Together, they fell into the underworld.

When they emerged under the cot in the school infirmary, Todd was ecstatic. "Imagine if there was a bed in every bank vault!"

Brian and Kiersten gave each other an exasperated look. They turned to leave, letting Todd follow them to the science classroom. There, Kiersten unlocked the supply cabinet.

Grabbing a sunlamp bulb off a shelf, Brian quickly went to work. He opened his backpack and pulled out a floodlight, a cigarette-lighter attachment, wire cutters, and a motorcycle battery.

With the wire cutters, he stripped the plug off the floodlight. Two wires dangled out. He attached them to the battery. Removing the floodlight from the socket, he replaced it with the sunlamp bulb. A Sun Gun, he decided to call it. He flicked the switch.

The room was drenched with brilliant white light. Todd and Kiersten covered their eyes.

And Brian felt himself stagger with pain.

Instantly he shut it off. Beads of cold sweat had formed on his forehead. A wave of nausea and fever passed through him, but he shook if off.

"Oh, man, that'll get them!" Todd exclaimed. "That's like a howitzer or something!"

Kiersten looked admiringly at Brian. "You must know a lot about electricity to do that."

Brian grinned modestly.

"So how come you get Fs in science?" she asked.

Brian's grin disappeared. He reached back into his pack, took out a newspaper, and checked the weather page. He looked down to the heading *SUNRISE/SUNSET*.

"What are you doing?" Kiersten asked.

Brian adjusted his wristwatch. "I'm setting my alarm for sunrise."

"What the heck for?" Todd piped up.

"When it beeps, we'll have three to five minutes," Brian said to him. "If we're not back up here before the sun clears the horizon, you and I turn into monsters."

Todd gulped. "Monsters? You mean there's a chance I might not make it?"

"Of course there's a chance!" Brian replied. "I'm pretty sure I know where Eric is, but I'm not leaving till I have him." He looked straight into Todd's eyes. "Are you still in? You don't have to."

Todd hesitated. His eyes fell to the ground as he thought it over. Finally he looked up, his face set with determination. "I'm in. Eric's my best friend."

Brian smiled. "Good, Todd. Let's go." Immediately the two boys ran for the door. "Thanks, Kiersten!" Brian called over his shoulder.

"Wait a second!" Kiersten shouted. "You're not leaving me behind. In the name of science, *I'm* going!"

The boys stopped in the doorway. Brian hadn't considered taking her — he figured she wouldn't want to go. But from the look on her face, she was dead serious.

"Okay," Brian said with a firm nod. "Let's do it."

There was no turning back now, Brian realized. If they got stuck, no one would ever find them.

He tried to keep that out of his mind as they ran to the infirmary and jumped into the shadow under the cot. But just before Brian's head disappeared, he took one last look around. This might be the last time he'd see the school.

As a human.

Chapter 19

Todd's face was filled with rapture. "It's a parallel dimension!" he shouted.

"Ssshh!" Brian warned.

"I might have a heart attack, I'm so happy," Todd said in a loud whisper.

Suddenly, in a flash of white, a monster jumped out of the shadows and grabbed Todd's backpack.

Todd screamed. Instantly Brian pulled a flashlight from his pack and shone the beam on the monster. In midair, it turned into a ball of clothes, rolling down the hall.

Brian kept the light trained on the pile as they approached it. Todd retrieved his backpack.

"Clothes," Kiersten said quietly, staring at the pile. "A lab coat."

"Sunlight kills them," Brian explained. "Artificial light turns them into clothes."

He clamped the light to the wall, keeping the beam aimed at the clothes. He reached into his bag and tossed Todd a light. "Todd, that's a two-cell double-D, with a supercharged thirty-five-watt krypton bulb. The finest light a Sears card can buy."

He threw another light to Kiersten. "That's a long-stem four-cell with a fifty-watt lamp and focus lens. Don't be afraid to use it."

For himself, he pulled out a hunting light. "Now, between the three of us we have plenty of firepower. If you see anything, nail it! Use your smaller lights to pin it. Ready?"

"Ready!" Kiersten replied.

For dramatic effect, Todd shone his light upward into his face. "Check! Let's turn this place into a Chinese laundry."

He was off to a good start. A blue robe fell to the floor at his feet.

Quickly Brian pinned it with his light. The three of them looked up. On a railing above them, shadows scurried around. Todd had accidentally zapped one of them.

"LIGHTS!" shrieked one of the monsters.

"Lights . . . lights . . . lights . . ." echoed others, their voices fading into the distance.

Brian cocked his light. Scanning left and right, he led the others forward.

With a *whoosh*, a glowing Frisbee whizzed past them.

"Bogies at two o'clock!" Todd yelled.

Flash. Brian turned an attacking monster into a tuxedo and top hat. He pinned it with a small flashlight.

Flash. Kiersten turned one into a wedding dress.

She took out a flashlight and pinned it.

Flash. Todd nailed a long gown and a mink stole, which flew onto Kiersten's shoulders. She smiled at her good fortune, angling her body to model it.

But Brian knocked it off her and pinned it. He smiled at Todd. "Fine shootin', Tex."

Todd grinned and blew on his light. "Piece of cake."

He spoke too soon. Three monsters appeared out of nowhere, taking aim with slingshots.

Ping! Ping! Ping! One by one, the lights were destroyed — the Sears special, the four-cell, and the hunting light. The monsters turned and fled.

Brian whipped out another flashlight. Flicking it on, he nailed one of the escaping attackers. The slingshot dropped to the floor.

All that was left now was the Sun Gun and a few flashlights. This was going to be even harder than Brian had thought. He tried to appear confident when he glanced at Kiersten and Todd. But he felt exactly the way they looked.

Scared.

By the time they got to the Monsterball field, their path was littered with piles of clothes. Each one was held in place by a beam from a clamped flashlight. The backpacks had become much lighter.

Brian and Kiersten stared at the field in awe. Lamps, TVs, stereos, and other expensive breakables glinted in the outfield. Beyond them, Snik's staircase loomed up into the sinister darkness.

"That's the master staircase," Brian said.

They walked toward it, taking a path through the outfield. Kiersten shook her head in amazement. "It's like Macy's down here!"

CRASHHH!

They dove behind a table as a baseball shattered a TV screen near them.

"Whatever happened to the good old-fashioned Nerf ball?" Todd remarked under his breath.

Without answering, Brian leaped up, brandishing a flashlight. But there wasn't a monster in sight. "Come on," he said to his friends.

They sprinted toward the staircase. With sudden, ear-shattering crashes, the outfield became a battlefield. Televisions exploded, fish tanks burst, mirrors cracked, and statues tumbled.

Dodging the shards of glass and metal, Brian, Todd, and Kiersten zigzagged their way to the bottom of the staircase.

And then, as suddenly as the noises had begun, they stopped. Brian looked over his shoulder.

Monsters surrounded the edges of the ballfield. Every one of them had his bat on his shoulder. Every one of them watched, with a strange, silent look of respect.

Brian swallowed hard. He knew why they were quiet. He knew why they'd stopped trying to kill.

They didn't have to anymore. Because anyone who got as far as the staircase was as good as dead.

Chapter 20

Brian, Todd, and Kiersten gazed up the staircase. Looming high above, the huge oak doors seemed to have a life of their own. Brian looked for signs of Snik, but he was nowhere to be seen.

Yet.

"How are we doing, Todd?" Brian asked.

Todd pulled the last two flashlights out of his pack, then threw the pack away. "Ready to rumble, sir."

"Kiersten?"

A flashlight in one hand, she flung her backpack over her shoulder. "Heavy artillery loss. One round left, sir."

Brian gave her the last flashlight in his pack. "Easy on the batteries. Let's go."

He reached his arm back and pulled out his master weapon — the customized Sun Gun. Clutching it tightly, he began the long trek upward.

As they approached, the doors began to move. Slowly, majestically, they swung open.

Brian's legs weakened. The room inside was immense. Dozens of free-standing shelves stretched across the floor, like a supermarket of toys gone out of control. Transformer robots spilled into boxes of Lincoln logs; erector sets and tinker toys sat next to blocks and spinning tops. Beyond the shelves, games of Monopoly and Parcheesi lay out on tables, ready to be played.

Ladders, slides, and swings were everywhere. And running among the shelves were train and race car tracks, crisscrossing from one side of the room to the other.

Another time, Brian might have thought he was in paradise. But right now he had a job to do. He stepped into the room with Todd and Kiersten.

The doors slammed behind them, echoing loudly.

Brian listened as the echo faded. He had never imagined seeing a place so crowded, yet so ominously empty. He looked across the room to see a grand staircase leading up to a balcony, which was supported below by high columns. Giant, closed jack-in-the-boxes lined the balcony. Behind them were three curtains.

His eyes widened as a massive black shadow rose against the curtains. Todd and Kiersten drew close to Brian. Together they stared upward, shoulder to shoulder.

The shadow moved forward. It was a human form. As it took steps, it expanded even larger, enveloping the balcony, until the figure itself was revealed.

Brian blinked. He couldn't believe his first glimpse. The treacherous, fearsome "Boy," the mention of whose name was enough to make every monster in the underworld quake with fear, was . . .

A *boy*!

A boy dressed in a neat blazer, a tie, shorts, and knee socks.

Brian could barely keep from laughing. This entire bizarre world was wrapped around the thumb of a good old American preppy kid! Somehow, in a strange way, it seemed fitting.

In Boy's right hand was a remote controller. He lifted it and pressed a button. A toy bear emerged from one of the shelves and started walking toward Brian.

Finally Boy spoke. "Brian Stevenson," he said. "The real Boy Wonder — at last. What a pleasure it is to make your acquaintance."

But Brian wasn't interested in small talk. "Where's Eric?" he demanded.

"And you brought some playmates along," he went on, ignoring the question. "Are they as tactful and fleet-footed as yourself? I daresay they don't look it."

"I want my brother!" Brian persisted.

"Now, Brian. What sort of greeting is that? After all, we are so much alike. If you stay, you'll be the one in charge of yourself. Perhaps this world, too — in time. You'll be the one with the power. The authority! Not your parents. Not your teachers.

You!" He smiled. "Isn't that what you want?"

The toy bear was inches away from Brian's foot. It rose up on its hind legs as if to shake hands.

"I want Eric — now!" Brian shouted.

Bzzzzzz. . . .

His eyes shifted downward. A rotating drill had popped out of the toy bear's snout. It lunged forward, boring the drill into Brian's shoe.

With a sudden kick, Brian propelled the bear across the room.

"Brian, why such cruelty?" Boy taunted. "You are such a unique individual. Your feats are unprecedented here. I can barely remember, if at all, the last time one of our breed has been trapped. Not once, but numerous times!"

Todd was growing impatient. "Enough wind, loafer breath," he said angrily. "Hand over the kid!"

"Very well," Boy replied. "Let's show the contestants what's behind curtain number one!"

Boy aimed his remote controller at the curtain. It opened, revealing a two-story-high dartboard.

Brian felt his jaw drop. Tied to the middle of the dartboard, his mouth gagged with a handkerchief, was Eric!

Chapter 21

Boy calmly picked out a dart from a set by his feet. He took aim at Eric.

"I'll make you a deal, Brian," he said. "It's your grace and wits I desire. Not those of your pugnacious chum or even your mute girlfriend. I'll let them all go *and* your brother if you'll stay and be my pal."

"No deals!" Brian answered.

Boy let the dart fly. With a sickening thump, it landed a millimeter from Eric's face.

"*Eriiiiic!*" Brian screamed, his heart pounding. He glared at Boy. "Let him go. Now! I'll give you ten seconds. Ten . . . nine . . . eight. . . ."

Boy threw another dart, just missing. "Be sensible," he said. "Why lose four lives when you can gain three? In an hour, you and your chums will be monsters, and then we all can play!"

"Seven . . . six . . . five. . . ."

"Let's blow him away, Brian!" Todd urged.

Brian pulled his Sun Gun around. Gripping it tightly, he cocked it at Boy. Beside him, Kiersten and Todd held up their lights.

With a swift, sure motion, Boy swept his remote controller in an arc, aiming at four jack-in-the-boxes. One by one, their cranks began to turn.

The tops sprung open, and out popped four guards. These were far more frightening than anything Brian had seen in the underworld.

It wasn't so much their shaved heads and ponytails, or the fact that they looked like trained Ninja warriors. It was that they were kids. Each and every one of them a boy or girl about Brian's age, with a face of twisted, snarling evil.

Brian wasn't going to let them stop his plan. "Four . . . three . . . let Eric go! . . . two . . . one!"

He pressed the trigger. A blinding streak of white light shot from the bulb. It caught one of the monster guards square in the chest. With a hair-raising shriek, he turned into clothes, then burst into flames.

Brian straightened out his aim, sending the light directly toward Boy.

Screaming in agony, Boy clutched his face and rolled to the ground.

Brian looked up to see a squadron of model planes swoop down from the ceiling, suspended by string. With perfect precision, they fired a barrage of bottle rockets.

Ping . . . SSMASSHHH! A rocket connected with the Sun Gun. It exploded in Brian's hands.

Ping! Ping! Kiersten's flashlight went up in smoke. *Ping!* One of Todd's lights was zapped out of his hand. He turned to fire the other one, but was hit in the arm. His second flashlight dropped to the floor.

Todd dove after his flashlight. He picked it up and looked at it. It was intact. Spinning around, he took aim — and came face to face with Snik!

He flicked the switch, but the bulb was dead.

Ignoring Todd, Snik reached for Brian's neck. Brian ducked away. "Run!" he shouted.

The three of them fanned out. Brian ran into an aisle between two toy shelves, followed by Snik. Todd tore off into another aisle, and Kiersten took a third.

The end of Kiersten's aisle disappeared into a menacing black void that seemed to beckon her. She stopped short and looked around.

Without warning, a monster guard leaped off a shelf. She madly rummaged through her pockets, then remembered a forgotten hiding place. Reaching down into her socks, she pulled out a penlight. She pointed it at the monster guard. "You're clothes, buddy!"

The monster guard collapsed into a heap of clothes. Kiersten felt relieved — but not for long. Below her, six buzzsaw blades split through the floor, tearing apart the clothes pile. They whirred slowly toward Kiersten. Defenseless, she moved closer and closer to the mysterious black void.

Todd fumbled with his flashlight. In his aisle, two monster guards kicked and slashed their way toward him like a team of Bruce Lees on fast-forward. As they came nearer, Todd whacked the flashlight against the shelf. Light poured out of it.

He looked at his attackers and shrugged casually. "With or without starch?" Flicking the light toward them, he turned the spinning warriors into two spinning uniforms.

But Todd's smile disappeared as toy tanks rumbled around the corner. A volley of bottle rockets shot toward him. One of them ripped the flashlight out of his hand.

Todd jumped back with a start. The monster guards rose from their heaps. As they moved toward him, spinning and chopping, he backed away into the darkness at the end of the aisle.

Brian was trapped against a wall. He could feel Snik's fiery breath on the back of his neck. He looked left and right at the stacks, crammed with toys. Only now did he notice that between the toys, he could see through to the next aisle.

He dove through the shelves to the other side. Scrambling to his feet, he put both hands on the stack and pushed.

Snik let out a grunt as he was buried under stuffed animals and Lincoln logs.

Now was Brian's chance. He dashed across the

floor toward the grand staircase. Behind him, tennis ball launchers rolled to the head of each aisle and fired.

Wham! A rocking horse turned to splinters as an exploding tennis ball hit it. *Wham! Wham! Wham!* Swing sets and sandboxes were destroyed.

Brian crumpled to the ground at the barrage. He staggered to his feet, weaving his way through the destruction. Reaching the staircase, he took the steps two at a time.

At the top, Boy was gone. Wisps of smoke rose from the smouldering remains of the zapped monster guard. Brian raced to curtain number one and pulled it open.

Nothing. No Eric, no dartboard.

He yanked curtain number two aside. It, too, was empty.

Then curtain number three. . . .

There was something there, all right.

Snik!

His overgrown hand grabbed Brian by the neck. Brian struggled to get loose.

Then, from behind the monster's hulking body, Boy emerged — or what was left of him. Where Brian's Sun Gun had hit his face, the skin had melted away. And what was underneath was not pretty.

Struggling in Snik's iron grip, Brian managed to let loose a kick to Boy's stomach. Boy flew backward onto the floor.

He picked himself up carefully, his half-face frowning with disappointment. "I was hoping we could be friends, Brian, but obviously you don't play fair."

"I haven't even started to play," Brian said through gritted teeth.

Boy's voice was chilling in its intensity. "You've misbehaved. You'll have to go to your room."

Snik lifted Brian up and held him over a deep black hole. Brian flailed desperately, but hung onto a faint hope. He had been in this situation before, and Maurice had rescued him.

But this time, Snik let go.

Brian plunged downward through the floor, screaming at the top of his lungs.

Chapter 22

"Well, Brian Stevenson, what now?"

Brian picked his head up to see Kiersten looking down at him. They had landed in what seemed to be a giant toy bin. He sat up and cast his eyes around. The floor was covered with stuffed animals. Old, useless, unwanted toys were piled everywhere.

Todd stood a few feet away, holding out an old-fashioned crank telephone. "Would you like to call 911 and request some backup?" he asked.

Brian had no time for jokes. "Is Eric here, anywhere?"

"Nope," Kiersten said. "Just you, me, Todd, and one useless door." She pointed to a corner of the room. A path had been cleared through the toys there, leading to a door with no handle.

"If only we had Snik to lend us his forehead," Todd remarked.

Brian went to the door and rammed it. It wouldn't budge. He ran his hands over every inch, looking for a weak spot. He looked at the gap under the door, which was only about a finger's width.

The thing was solid. There was no way they'd get through.

"Where's our guardian angel when we need him?" Todd said.

A muffled "Oooooo" arose from a mound of toys behind them. Brian turned and grabbed a rubber sword. Todd picked up a bow and arrow. Kiersten snatched a dart gun.

The mound slowly moved. Kiersten fired a dart. Brian prepared to charge with his sword.

And as Todd let loose with an arrow, Maurice emerged from the pile.

Thwwwock! The arrow's rubber suction cup connected squarely with Maurice's forehead. It dangled limply as Maurice staggered backward. His eyes were puffy, his body bruised, his clothes torn and stained with food.

"Maurice!" Brian shouted. "What happened?"

"What happened?" Maurice pulled the arrow off his forehead and glowered at Todd. "Two inches lower and that bonehead would have a lawsuit on his hands!"

Kiersten and Todd dropped their weapons. "You know him?" Todd asked in utter shock. "He's a monster!"

Brian nodded.

"A monster . . ." Kiersten repeated, her eyes fixed on something in a toy pile. "I have an idea!"

Kiersten grabbed the phone, a swiss army knife,

and two pencils. The others watched as she pulled wires from the bottom of the phone, then shaved the ends off the pencils with the knife. "It's the same principle as the carbon lamp in a movie projector," she explained.

"Right. Lights from pencils," Maurice said dryly. "And I'm the Pope. Red, are you sure *you're* not part light bulb?"

Kiersten sneered at him, then quickly gave Brian instructions. He hooked a battery to the phone. Then he took the two phone wires and connected them to a sharpened end of each pencil.

Kiersten gave Todd the phone. "Todd, you turn the crank. Brian, touch the points of the pencils together, then slowly pull them apart." Then she gave Maurice a look. "I'll slide the dirty laundry under the door."

Stinging from the remark, Maurice stood by the door. Todd began to crank. Brian did as he was told. Absolutely nothing happened.

Maurice rolled his eyes.

"Faster, Todd," Kiersten said.

Todd cranked harder. Smirking, Maurice chanted, "Go, Toad, go! Go, Toad, go!"

Todd scowled at him. "Faster!" Brian shouted.

"I'm *trying*!" Todd retorted.

"Right," Maurice jeered. "I've seen monkey grinders crank faster."

With an angry burst, Todd whipped the crank around. Suddenly a spark shot across the pencil tips. The spark grew into a light — a harsh, white light. . . .

Maurice's body evaporated. Kiersten slid the clothes to the door and tried to stuff them underneath.

Sweat poured from Todd's forehead. His arm began to tire. The bright light began to flicker, then slowly dim. Kiersten feverishly fed the clothes through the crack, inch by inch.

Then the light petered out. Instantly Maurice sprang to life, protruding through the door from the waist up. His face was contorted with agony. "CRANK, YOU FOOL!" he shrieked. "CRANK!"

With a burst of strength, Todd cranked furiously. Maurice became clothes again, and Kiersten jammed him through.

Exhausted, Todd dropped the phone and collapsed.

From outside the door there was a crash, a small yelp of pain, and silence.

"Open the door, Maurice . . ." Brian said.

There was more silence, then some grunts and groans. Finally Maurice's voice came through the door.

"Any of you freaks know how to pick a combination lock?"

Brian slumped. Kiersten groaned. Todd buried his head in his hands.

There was no question now. They were doomed.

Chapter 23

Brian scanned the room for ideas. Without Maurice, escape was going to be next to impossible —

With a sudden crash, the door burst open. Maurice leered at them with a wide, ugly grin. "Got you scared, huh?"

Brian didn't even respond. He rushed past Maurice and out into a hallway.

"Where are you going?" Todd called out.

"We need more firepower!" Brian yelled over his shoulder.

The sound of speeding footsteps echoed in the underworld as the four of them raced away.

In no time, Brian, Todd, and Kiersten were out of the monster world and in the school supply closet again.

"Where's Maurice?" Todd whispered, grabbing every light he could from the shelves.

"Don't worry about him," Brian said, frantically

helping Kiersten splice wires together. "He's paying a visit to an old friend."

From the bottom shelf, Todd dragged out several enormous car batteries. He pushed aside dozens of flashlights, floodlights, and headlights that were strewn about the floor.

Todd watched in awe as the other two connected up the lights in a complex pattern. He had no idea what they were up to. If they expected to tote all this stuff into the underworld, who was going to carry the batteries? They must have weighed close to a ton.

But for the first time in his life, Todd just did what he was told and didn't ask any questions.

The monster world was like a ghost town as they walked across the Monsterball field. Not one of them was scared — not with the getups they were wearing. On their three heads were three helmets, each containing a floodlight and two flashlights. From neck to waist, they bulged with more lights. Lights pointing forward, lights pointing sideways, round lights, square lights.

Brian looked behind him to check his power supply. His eyes followed the main feeder cable to a massive wooden tray stacked with car batteries — nestled in the beefy arms of Ronnie Coleman!

Maurice had his arm around Ronnie's shoulder. They both gave Brian a reassuring wink.

Somehow, Brian had known that those two would hit it off.

Their sneakers touching lightly on the steps, they all ascended the master staircase. They scurried across the toy-filled room and started a slow climb to Boy's balcony.

The stairs creaked below them, echoing through the chamber. On the balcony, the three curtains hung open, revealing three small empty stages.

"You better take cover, Maurice," Brian whispered.

Maurice disappeared down the stairs. The others readied themselves, taking the steps one by one. . . .

Suddenly they stopped. With an explosion of noise, Boy's weapons went berserk. Monster guards popped out of their boxes. Toy attack planes dropped from the sky. Tennis-ball launchers fired.

Ronnie dropped the tray of batteries and picked up a set of jumper cable clamps. He stood ready.

Above them, two familiar shadows approached. As Boy appeared over the ledge, with Snik at his side, he smiled scornfully.

Until he saw them.

For the first time, Brian caught a glimpse of something he never thought he'd see on Boy's face.

Fear.

"What the — ?" Boy muttered.

"Say good night, Boy!" Brian said.

He signaled to Ronnie. Ronnie clamped the jumper cables. Sparks spurted into the air.

There was an explosion of light, like an atomic blast without the noise. It felt as if they'd jumped into the center of the sun. What was black became white.

And what was a monster became history.

The monster guard went up in flames. Snik burst apart, sending tiny swatches of cloth floating in the air.

And Boy's face, contorted with agony, melted into itself. Brian watched in awe as it exploded into a blue flame.

The flame began to consume Boy's entire body. His clothes slowly crumpled to the floor, into a neat, perfectly folded pile. Then they, too, ignited, leaving only a charred circle.

First part of the mission accomplished. Now it was time to find Eric.

Brian, Todd, and Kiersten began tearing off their bulbs. Ronnie disconnected the jumper cables. Around them, the tiny scraps of Snik's clothing were falling like a silent snow flurry.

Beep!

Brian felt a jolt of panic. It was the warning signal from his watch.

"We gotta get out of here!" Todd shouted.

Todd was right. They were minutes away from turning into permanent monsters. If they ran, they *might* have a chance of returning. But there was one problem.

Brian wasn't going anywhere without Eric.

Chapter 24

Brian raced down the stairs. "Eric's here some-where, I know it!" He threw toys aside, wiping shelves clear with his arms.

Like rats, he and Todd and Kiersten and Ronnie rummaged through the room.

Near the oak doors, out of sight, pieces of Snik's clothing fell into a pile. Gradually they started to move, fusing together . . . forming part of a foot, then a leg. . . .

Meanwhile Brian scooted up the stairs to the bal-cony. He ran past Boy's burning clothes, looking desperately for clues.

Suddenly he stopped. There was a muffled noise — somewhere. He looked around, but there was no sign of life.

No sign, that is, except for the jerky movements of a jack-in-the-box.

It was the only one that hadn't opened before. The only one that hadn't let loose a whirling, ruth-less monster guard.

Brian inched closer. Could it possibly be Eric? If it was a monster guard, Brian was a goner. Without any lights, there was no defense.

He crept up to it. Sweat ran in rivulets down his neck. He reached for the top and tried to pry it open. It was stuck. He found the crank and turned it.

Music filled the room. It was tinkling and innocent, and the most frightening sound Brian had ever heard. Out of the corner of his eye, he spotted Kiersten, Todd, and Ronnie running up the stairs.

Wonnnng! The top sprang open. Brian fell backward.

It was Eric! Brian threw his arms around him. "Let's go!" he yelled, through a relieved smile.

They barreled down the stairs. Trampling over piles of toys, they turned a corner toward the oak doors — and froze in their tracks.

There was a major obstacle in their way — Snik. Or at least three quarters of him. Before their eyes he was reforming, his muscles already flexing in preparation to destroy.

"How much time?" Kiersten asked.

"Maybe a minute," Brian replied.

"Great," Todd said. "Coleman, can you take him?"

Ronnie backed away, his face chalk-white.

"Who is that guy?" Eric asked.

From the bottom of the master staircase, behind Snik, came Maurice's voice. "Hey, Snik!"

Snik's partially formed body turned. Brian, Eric,

Todd, Kiersten, and Ronnie peered down the stairs.

At the bottom, Maurice cheerfully held up a blow-torch. "Say, Snik, how about a light?"

Maurice braced himself and aimed. A powerful flame roared up the staircase.

With a yell that seemed to well up from his toes, Snik caught fire. He sank to the floor, crumbling like an old log.

Brian led the others in a race across the Monsterball field. All around them, monsters began to appear. Only this time they were cheering, egging Brian on.

The four kids and Maurice flew through the underworld, passing stairway after stairway. Brian felt the strain of every muscle. Finally they got to the Stevensons'. Brian leaped onto it and climbed three steps at a time. Above him, the blackness got closer — the blackness he had so easily passed through before.

He raised his hand above his head as he ran. He watched it thrust through the darkness.

And he was filled with terror when it hit a solid, unmovable barrier!

Chapter 25

Hauling his arm back, he punched the barrier.

Maurice pushed past Brian. He reached up and tried it himself.

It was no use. Even he couldn't get through.

"It's too late," Maurice said sadly.

Eric stared at him in disbelief. "What does that mean?"

"It means we've dissected our last frog," Todd answered. "We're stuck. We're monsters."

Ronnie nodded. "I can handle that."

There was an awkward silence. They all sat down. Eric looked at his feet.

Then, in choked little bursts, Kiersten began to sob. Brian looked around. Five pairs of eyes were cast to the ground, all five of them wet.

We blew it, Brian thought. We were late by a minute, and we blew it.

He sighed. If only the earth had given them a break — stopped rotating, or even slowed down a bit. Now the morning sun was peeking over New

England, and that was that. There was no going back.

Or was there. . . ?

"Well, Ronnie, *I* can't handle it," he finally said. He jumped to his feet. "Follow me."

"Where are you going?" Maurice cried out.

Brian streaked down the hallway. He climbed ladders, slid down chutes. Behind him, he could hear the clatter of the others' footfalls. Signs whizzed past them: Pittsburgh, Indianapolis, St. Louis. . . .

Brian darted up a stairway. The huffing and puffing of the others echoed in the darkness as he paused at the top. He tried to put his hand through but couldn't.

"Sun's up in St. Louis," he said.

Sprinting back down, he led the expedition farther west. His legs pumped madly as his sneakers pounded the floor. There were more signs: Wichita, Santa Fe, Phoenix. A monster stumbled down the Phoenix staircase, his back sizzling. With an embarrassed grin, he said, "Sun's up."

They kept going, until Maurice pulled to a stop in front of another stairway. "Here," he said.

He went up first and reached into the darkness.

When Maurice's face lit up, Brian knew his hand had gone through.

Brian ran up next to him. Together they helped Ronnie, Kiersten, Todd, and Eric scramble up through the hole.

Then it was Brian's turn. He looked up, but didn't follow the rest.

Instead, he turned to Maurice. "I — I kind of wish I could stay."

"You'd be a hero down here," Maurice said.

Brian looked away shyly.

Maurice sighed. "But I suppose you'll be getting married soon."

"Married?" Brian gave him a baffled look. "To whom?"

"To the light bulb! You know — Red!"

"Kiersten? No *way*! Just friends."

Maurice nodded understandingly, but Brian could see a mischievous glint in his eye. Brian felt his face turning red. He had to admit Kiersten wasn't bad, for a girl. . . .

"Well, I guess that's what it's all about," Maurice said.

"I guess." Brian gave him a broad smile. "And you know what? You're the best friend I ever had."

Maurice grinned and wrapped him in a hug. "You're the ugliest friend I ever had."

Brian wasn't sure, but he thought he saw a tear start to form in one of Maurice's eyes. He began to head up into the darkness. "I'm going to miss you, Maurice. I really am."

"Wait a minute!" Maurice called out. "Wait a dog-gone minute! Are you going to stop sleeping in a bed?"

"No."

"So then I'll be seeing you." Maurice put his hands on his hips. "Bri baby, just 'cause you tiptoed down here and threw the wildest bash this town has ever seen, it doesn't in any way exclude you from catching your share of *trouble*!"

"Trouble? What about my arm? It turned to clothes last night!"

"Don't worry, you'll sleep it off. Nothing's permanent unless you're trapped down here."

Todd's voice wafted down from above them. "Let's go, Brian, the sun's coming up. I'm not running to Hawaii!"

Brian started back up again.

"Hang on," Maurice said. He yanked off his jacket and tossed it to Brian.

Brian caught it and smiled. "Hey, you don't have to — "

"Relax, I'll find another." Maurice shrugged. "Maybe I'll even steal it back from you."

"Come on, Brian!" came Eric's voice.

" 'Bye, Maurice," Brian said.

"Take care, Kimosabe," Maurice answered. "And always remember — where there's a bed, there's a way!"

Brian chuckled. Then, stepping up the stairway, he disappeared into the room above.

As he passed through the shadow, he caught a strong ocean breeze. A small clump of wet sand flew into his mouth. He looked up — and realized he was under the plastic mesh of an outdoor lounge chair.

In the distance, waves crashed against the shore.

Some "room."

Brian climbed out onto a vast beach. A few feet away, Kiersten, Eric, Todd, and Ronnie stood staring out over a dune.

He walked up beside them. Silently they watched the massive orange sun peek over the horizon. In the sudden heat, the morning air seemed to quiver.

And for the first time in two days, the sight of the sunrise filled Brian with strength.

As they walked to a pay phone, they passed a sign that read MALIBU BEACH. Brian picked up the receiver.

But before he dialed, he turned to his friends. "Uh, Kiersten? Your science project. . . . And Ronnie, about that sandwich. I want you both to know . . ." He took a deep breath and held back a smile. "Maurice did it."

Quickly he dialed his parents. "Hello?" came his mother's anxious voice.

"Hi, Mom," he said.

"Brian?"

"Mom, I found Eric."

"My God, are you both all right?" she gasped.

"Yeah, we're fine."

He heard a muffled voice in the background. Then his mom continued, "Honey, I want you to stay right where you are. Your dad is here. He's walking out the door right now to come and pick you up."

"But — "

"Okay, where are you?"

"Mom, I know it sounds crazy, but we're in Malibu."

"Malibu, Massachusetts. . . ?"

"Where on earth is that?" came Mr. Stevenson's voice in the background.

"No, Mom," Brian said calmly. "Malibu, California."

There was a momentary silence. "*Malibu . . . California? What are you doing there?*"

"Here, let me talk to him," his father's voice interrupted. "Brian, this is your father!" he barked. "Are you sure you're all right?"

"Yes, Dad."

"Is Eric there?"

"Yes, Dad."

"Is there someone else I might be able to talk to?"

A helpless smile crept across Brian's face. "Dad," he said slowly, "you're not going to believe this. . . ."

Kiersten, Eric, Todd, and Ronnie were shaking, trying not to laugh out loud.

Brian took a deep breath. He had a feeling this was going to be a long, long day.